D0051668

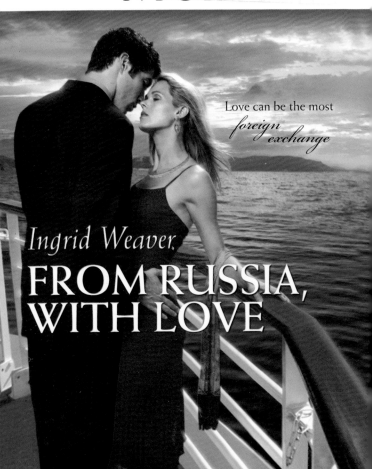

Love can be the most
foreign
exchange

Ingrid Weaver

FROM RUSSIA, WITH LOVE

HARLEQUIN®

Mediterranean NIGHTS™

Escape to the glamorous world of cruising with the guests
and crew of *Alexandra's Dream*—the newest luxury ship
to set sail on the romantic Mediterranean Sea.

Each book in the
Mediterranean Nights
series is packed with intrigue,
deception, adventure and romance.

ISBN-13:978-0-373-38960-5
ISBN-10: 0-373-38960-4

Collect all 12!

 EAN

WHERE DREAMS COME TRUE

The Daily Cruise Letter/The Daily Cruise News

The Master of *Alexandra's Dream,* Captain Nick Pappas, welcomes you on board Liberty Line's premier ship. Experience the glamour and elegance of cruising at its best as we sail through the beautiful waters of the Mediterranean.

Book a shore excursion to the site of the first Olympics, explore the cobbled streets of Dubrovnik and shop the markets of Naples. To learn more about the treasures of ancient Greece and Rome, see librarian Ariana Bennett for information on a special lecture series by Father Patrick Connelly.

We hope you'll make yourself comfortable on this luxurious ship. Enjoy fine dining in the Empire Room, a cup of tea in the Rose Petal tearoom, the best wines in La Belle Epoque and chocolate to die for in Temptations Café. And after a late-night show in the Poseidon Lounge, make your way to the observation deck for the best entertainment of all—a little stargazing on a Mediterranean night.

Adventure, romance and relaxation. You'll find it all on board *Alexandra's Dream,* and our staff is here to help make it happen.

Have a wonderful trip!

INGRID WEAVER's

writing career evolved from her irrepressible imagination, her love of reading...and from her fondness for comfortable clothes. The bestselling author of more than twenty books, she has won the Romance Writers of America RITA® Award for Romantic Suspense and the *Romantic Times BOOKreviews* Career Achievement Award for Series Romantic Suspense. Ingrid lives on a farm near Toronto, where she's currently at work on her next novel. You can visit Ingrid's Web site at www.ingridweaver.com.

Mediterranean NIGHTS™

Ingrid Weaver

FROM RUSSIA, WITH LOVE

HARLEQUIN®

TORONTO • NEW YORK • LONDON
AMSTERDAM • PARIS • SYDNEY • HAMBURG
STOCKHOLM • ATHENS • TOKYO • MILAN • MADRID
PRAGUE • WARSAW • BUDAPEST • AUCKLAND

ISBN-13: 978-0-373-38960-5
ISBN-10:   0-373-38960-4

FROM RUSSIA, WITH LOVE

Copyright © 2007 by Harlequin Books S.A.

Ingrid Weaver is acknowledged as the author of this work.

www.eHarlequin.com

Printed in U.S.A.

Dear Reader,

Start with a tall, handsome man and a passionate woman. Add a luxury cruise ship and the picturesque Mediterranean Sea. Mix in ten carefree days and romantic nights. Sounds like a recipe for smooth sailing, doesn't it?

Not quite. Not when the woman involved is Marina Artamova, a flamboyant Russian fashion designer whose sole reason for taking the cruise is to gain custody of her orphaned nephew. More than any other character I've created over the years, Marina seemed to spring from the page fully formed the instant I began to write. I admire her determination and her fearless honesty (although I must admit I do envy her fashion sense). And being a mother myself, I fell a little in love with her hero, David Anderson, the devoted adoptive father who will do anything to keep his new son. It was tough to put them through the emotional wringer of a custody dispute—how could I choose which side wins when both sides are right?

Simple. I added another side. A deadly one.

Of course, I've always preferred my romance seasoned with a generous helping of danger. When I was invited to participate in the MEDITERRANEAN NIGHTS series and set a story on a ship, I thought of both *The Love Boat* and Steven Seagal's *Under Siege*. I hope you enjoy *From Russia, With Love*. It was a sheer pleasure to write.

Best wishes,

Ingrid

To Marsha Zinberg, our intrepid skipper,
and to the crew of *Mediterranean Nights*.

DON'T MISS THE STORIES OF

Mediterranean
N I G H T S™

PROLOGUE

Near Murmansk, Russia
August, one year ago

THE GORSKY FAMILY car was barely large enough for two adults and a child. It was rusted through in some places and held together with wire in others. And while the engine was temperamental to start and rattled when it got going, traveling anywhere was an adventure for Stefan. It meant his father had sold his catch and had brought his boat home, and for the next few days his mother would sing while she made breakfast, even though she and his father took a lot of naps. And once his parents weren't so tired anymore, Stefan's father would pull the tarp off the car and announce they all deserved a holiday.

They seldom went far. On warm days they drove to the round rocks near the seashore for a picnic with beet salad and boiled eggs. Other times they went to the harbor, where Stefan watched the ships from his special perch high above the world on his father's shoulders.

No matter where they went, coming home was always the same. Stefan's mother would smile and squeeze close to his father in the front seat while Stefan curled up in the back with his toys and his blanket, lulled to sleep by the sound of his parents' whispered laughter and the hum of the tires.

But this trip wasn't like the others. The Gorsky family had packed clothes instead of a picnic, and darkness had fallen yet they hadn't started back. The car was going faster than it ever had, making the body shudder and the engine smoke, but that wasn't enough for Stefan's father. Borya rocked back and forth while he gripped the wheel, as if he was trying to make the car go even faster. Olena kept twisting to look behind them. Headlights glared through the rain that streaked the rear windshield, casting watery shadows that mingled with the tears on her face.

Stefan rubbed his blanket against his cheek and pushed his thumb into his mouth. His mother was yelling, her voice shaking with words he couldn't understand. His father should have taken the deal, done what they'd asked. These people were too powerful. His pride would get them killed.

There was a string of popping sounds. The rear windshield shattered, showering Stefan with beads of glass. Olena shouted at her son to get on the floor as Borya wrenched the wheel, sending the car skidding across the road.

Stefan half slid, half fell from the seat to the floor. Crumbs of glass clung to his blanket, glittering like ice in the glare of the headlights. He was crying now, his breath coming in hiccups, and banging his fist into his nose so he had to let go of his thumb. He grabbed his toy boat and hugged it to his chest. He wanted this trip to end. He wanted his mother to stop screaming and sing again, and he wanted his father to lift him high on his shoulders, so high, until he could touch the clouds....

The end came swiftly. The little car that was the pride of the Gorsky family was no match for the heavy sedan that pursued it. Through the gaping hole where the rear windshield had been came the roar of an engine. The first hit knocked Stefan into the back of his mother's seat. The next propelled the car off the road and spiraling through the air.

Stefan was thrown clear on the first roll and landed in a loganberry bush. He couldn't cry—the impact had knocked his breath from his body—so he didn't make a sound as he saw the car slam upside-down into the far side of the ditch.

Headlights carved through the rain as the sedan that had hit them swung around in the middle of the road. It had barely come to a halt when a man in a long black coat emerged and ran to the wreck. Apart from one tire that was still spinning and the steam that rose from the front end, nothing moved in the mass of metal. There was no sound, either. Stefan's mother was no longer screaming.

The man in black walked all around the car, bent over to look inside, then straightened and spat on it. Squinting against the rain, he drew a gun from his coat and peered into the darkness beyond the headlights. "Come out, little boy," he called. "I won't hurt you."

Stefan's breath returned on a sob. His throat ached, the stiff branches of the loganberry bush were pricking him through his shirt and the rain was making him shiver. Tears burned his eyes with the need to cry, but terror kept him silent.

That must be a monster, not a man. His coat flapped behind him like wings. His eyes were black beads, and a white line like a sickle gleamed in the rain that pelted his cheek. Monsters ate little boys. That's what the stories said.

So Stefan did the only thing a four-year-old could.

He ran.

CHAPTER ONE

Piraeus, Greece
May, nine months later

"THERE SHE IS, Stefan. *Alexandra's Dream*." David Anderson squatted beside his new son and pointed at the dark blue hull that towered above the pier. The cruise ship was a majestic sight, twelve decks high and as long as a city block. A circle of silver and gold stars, the logo of the Liberty cruise line, gleamed from the swept-back smokestack. Like some legendary sea creature born for the water, the ship emanated power from every sleek curve. Even at rest it held the promise of motion. "That's going to be our home for the next ten days."

The child beside him remained silent, his cheeks working in and out as he sucked furiously on his thumb. Hair so blond it appeared white ruffled against his forehead in the harbor breeze. The baby-sweet scent unique to the very young mingled with the tang of the sea.

"Ship," David said. "Uh, *parakhod*."

From beneath his bangs, Stefan looked at *Alexandra's Dream*. Although he didn't release his thumb, the corners of his mouth tightened with the beginning of a smile.

David grinned. That was Stefan's first smile this afternoon, one of only two since they had left the orphanage yesterday. It was probably because of the boat. According to the orphanage staff, the boy loved boats, which was the main reason David had decided to book this cruise. Then again, there was a strong possibility the smile could have been a reaction to David's attempt at pocket-dictionary Russian. Whatever the cause, it was a good start.

The liaison from the adoption agency had claimed that Stefan had been taught some English, but David had yet to see evidence of it. David continued to speak, positive his son would understand his tone even if he couldn't grasp the words. "This is her maiden voyage. Her first trip, just like this is our first trip, and that makes it special." He motioned toward the stage that had been set up on the pier beneath the ship's bow. "That's why everyone's celebrating."

The ship's official christening ceremony had been held the day before and had been a closed affair, with only the cruise line executives and VIP guests invited, but the stage hadn't yet been disassembled. Banners bearing the blue and white of the Greek flag, as well as the Liberty circle of stars logo, draped the edges of the platform. In the center, a group of musicians and a dance troupe dressed in traditional white folk costumes performed for the benefit of the ship's first passengers. Their audience was in a festive mood, snapping their fingers in time to the music while the dancers twirled and wove through their steps.

David bobbed his head to the rhythm of the mandolins. The musicians were playing a folk tune that seemed vaguely familiar, possibly from a movie he'd seen. He hummed a few notes. "Catchy melody, isn't it?"

Stefan turned his gaze on David. His eyes were a striking shade of blue, as cool and pale as a winter horizon and far too solemn for a child not yet five. Still, the smile that hovered at the corners of his mouth persisted. He moved his head with the music, mirroring David's motion.

David gave a silent cheer at the interaction. He hoped this cruise would provide countless opportunities for more. "Hey, good for you," he said. "Do you like the music?"

The child's eyes sparked. He withdrew his thumb with a pop. *"Moozika!"*

"Music. Right!" David held out his hand. "Come on, let's go closer so we can watch the dancers."

Stefan grasped David's hand quickly, as if he feared it would be withdrawn. In an instant his budding smile was replaced by a look close to panic.

David squeezed the boy's fingers and leaned in to give him a hug. He was tempted to scoop the boy into his arms and tickle him until he giggled, just the way he did with his nieces and nephews back home, but he knew better than to push things. Their relationship was only beginning. Trust couldn't be forced, it had to be earned, especially with a child who had gone through all that Stefan had.

Did he remember the car accident that had killed his parents? It would be a mercy if he didn't. As far as David knew, Stefan had never spoken of it to anyone. Whatever he had seen had made him run so far from the crash that the police hadn't found him until the next day. The event had traumatized him to the extent that he hadn't uttered a word until his fifth week at the orphanage. Even now, he seldom talked.

David sat back on his heels and brushed the hair from Stefan's forehead. That solemn, too-old gaze locked with his, and for an instant David felt as if he looked back in time at an image of himself thirty years ago.

He didn't need to speak the same language to understand exactly how this boy felt. He knew what it meant to be alone and powerless among strangers, trying to be brave and tough but wishing with every fiber of his being for a place to belong, to be safe, and most of all for someone to love him....

Stefan had scars on his feet because he'd lost his shoes when he'd run from the crash. David had scars on his back because he'd had nowhere to run. Yet it was the other scars, the wounds no one else could see, that hurt the most and took the longest to heal. David understood that, too.

He knew in his heart he would be a good parent to Stefan. It was the reason he had never considered halting the adoption process after Ellie had left him. He hadn't balked when he'd learned of the recent claim by Stefan's spinster aunt, either: the absentee relative had shown up too late for her case to be considered. The adoption was meant to be. He and this child already shared a bond that went deeper than paperwork or legalities.

A seagull screeched overhead, making Stefan start and press closer to David.

"That's my boy," David murmured. He swallowed hard, struck by the simple truth of what he had just said.

That's my boy.

"BUT STEFAN'S NOT *his* child. He can't be." Marina Artamova shook back her bracelets and crammed her phone to her ear as she wove through the crowd in the cruise terminal. "How could things have gone so far? This is all a terrible mistake."

"Marina, calm down. You're not listening to me. I said in the eyes of the law, Stefan is considered David Anderson's son. The adoption has already gone through."

Marina fought against the urge to throw her phone. Her lawyer was emotionless and methodical, everything she wasn't, which was why she'd hired him. From the time her career had begun to flourish, he'd served her well, navigating the maze of international law as competently as he handled her Moscow traffic tickets. But his insistence on playing by the rules this time was frustrating. "Rudolph, it's not one of my designs that has been stolen, it's my sister's child."

"Stefan wasn't stolen. All the correct procedures were followed."

"How could they have been? His name was spelled wrong. That's why I couldn't find him. Or maybe I couldn't find him because those greedy commissars at the adoption agency didn't want to lose their fat fees from the American. Did you think of that?"

"Marina, although I do admire your flair for the dramatic, as far as I know there was no conspiracy here. It was merely incompetence. Our welfare system is overburdened and underfunded, so mistakes are not uncommon."

"Is this why you called me? To tell me there is nothing you can do?"

"Quite the contrary. I've found a judge who will hear our petition next week."

She scrutinized the line of passengers at the check-in, just in case David Anderson and Stefan hadn't already gone through. The people she saw ran the gamut from clusters of gray-haired vacationers to couples who were probably honeymooners, judging by the way they stood entwined with each other. There were several couples with children in tow, but there was no sign of her blond nephew or the man who had stolen him. "They're leaving today, Rudolph."

"Yes, I'm aware of that. We've known their itinerary for a week. It can't be helped. Our only recourse is to wait for the court to reverse the adoption."

"Do you expect me to be satisfied with that? He's my nephew. My godson. He doesn't need some stranger, a divorced foreigner, he needs *me*...." Her voice broke on the last word. She dug through her shoulder bag in search of a tissue, then gave up and grabbed the end of her silk scarf instead. "I owe it to my sister," she said, blotting her eyes with the scarf. "I know we had our differences, but she would want me to raise him."

"I assure you, the judge will take all of this into account. Be patient, Marina."

She gave the check-in line one last look, then scowled at the white-suited cruise company personnel who manned the desk. A few of them were snapping their fingers and one was dancing in place to the rhythm of the Greek folk music that was coming through the speakers behind the counter. Apparently they were celebrating the ship's launch. *Alexandra's Dream* had been completely refurbished and carried high expectations, so everyone except Marina was in a party mood. She gave her eyes another swipe and flipped her scarf over her shoulder. "I can't be patient, Rudolph. I'm not going to stand by and watch my nephew get ripped from his country and his roots to live on the other side of the world."

Rudolph hissed out a slow breath. "Marina, I don't like the sound of that. What are you planning?"

"I'm going to talk some sense into this American kidnapper."

"No. Absolutely not. As I already advised you, we'll handle this through the courts. Any direct contact with

Anderson might give him ammunition his lawyer could use against you later."

"Once he hears my side, we won't need the courts."

"Marina, leave this to me. No offence, but diplomacy is not your strong suit."

"Diplomacy be damned. Their ship's due to sail at five o'clock."

"Then you wouldn't have an opportunity to speak with him even if his lawyer agreed to a meeting."

"I'll have ten days of opportunities, Rudolph, since I plan to be on board that ship."

"Marina!"

"I'll call you tomorrow with an update." She terminated the connection to cut off the protest she knew was coming and shoved the phone into her bag. She would let the lawyers worry about the legalities; her only worry was the child. She unzipped the compartment that held her papers. Her hand shook as she withdrew her ticket.

It had been outrageously expensive to obtain last-minute passage on *Alexandra's Dream,* but her money had to be good for something besides keeping her accountant in sable and paying Rudolph's exorbitant fees.

Olena had never wanted any part of her younger sister's wealth. It had been yet another source of the friction between them. Whenever Marina had offered money to make her sister's life easier, Olena had laughed and said she had all the riches she could wish for. She had a husband who loved her and a son she adored. No amount of rubles could buy that.

She'd been right. Olena and Borya had been the happiest couple Marina had ever seen. God, it was hard to believe they were gone.

Would they still be alive if Marina had tried harder to help them? She should have gone home more often. Or she should have persuaded them to move to Moscow and work for her—she would have found something they could do. At the very least she should have overruled Borya's pride and bought him a new car. She kept telling them that old heap was a death trap....

The scene before her wavered. Marina blinked the tears away and headed for the check-in. She had plenty of regrets, but this was no time to indulge them. The nightmare was nearing its end. The grief and frustration of her nine-month-long search were almost over.

That's why she didn't give a damn what Rudolph or the law said. She wasn't going to let anyone keep Stefan from her now.

MIKE O'CONNOR BREATHED a silent sigh of relief as he passed through the last security check and walked on board. This job was almost too good to be true, an entire summer of getting paid to meander around the Mediterranean on a luxury cruise ship. It was a taste of the good life that he intended to continue. Once he finished here he'd be able to retire to someplace tropical where the drinks were cheap and the women wore even less than those little umbrellas that decorated the booze.

Someone knocked into him from behind. He clamped his jaw on the curse that rose to his lips and reminded himself to stay in character.

"Oh, Father, I'm sorry. I wasn't watching where I was going."

The voice was female, heavily accented and as rich as dark rum. Mike had a quick mental image of beaches and skimpy bikinis as he turned, but the tall woman who stood in front of him wasn't anywhere near as inviting as her voice. She had a spectacular mane of blond hair, but the rest of her looked hands-off. "It's quite all right, my dear," he said, putting on a bland smile. "We're all eager to get started on our journey."

"Yes, of course." She blinked quickly a few times and scanned the crowd in the corridor around them. Her eyes were red.

Hell, was she crying? The priest's identity that he'd assumed for this gig was great for a cover. It had been his ticket to a free ride, and as a guest lecturer, he could move around the ship as freely as the crew, but staying in character might prove to be a nuisance. Getting involved with any of the passengers' problems was the last thing he wanted. Still, a priest's job was to comfort. "You appear troubled. Are you looking for someone?"

"Yes, as a matter of fact, I am. My nephew. He has blond hair and would be about this tall." Silver bracelets tinkled at her wrist as she gestured to indicate a child's height. "Have you seen him?"

Mike shook his head, trying to project the appropriate mixture of concern and sympathy, but he wasn't listening anymore. "I'm sorry. Perhaps one of the cruise staff could assist you."

She nodded and moved toward the open deck, her gaze darting over the crowd.

Mike caught the flash of cameras from the corner of his eye and automatically averted his face. The caution was unnecessary, though, since the photographer's attention was on a gray-haired man who was posing with a pair of much younger women. From the looks of them, they could have been his daughters.

Mike recognized the man from the homework he'd done. It was Elias Stamos himself, the Greek shipping magnate who had recently acquired this ship, along with the other two in the Liberty line. Even at sixty-five the Stamos family patriarch was an imposing figure, tanned and fit, with an aggressive bearing that made him appear taller than he actually was. Mike had heard he was as unyielding in his personal standards as he was in his business affairs, and his reputation as a Greek patriot and patron of the arts was beyond reproach.

Which made *Alexandra's Dream* perfect for Mike's purpose. No one would suspect a thing. The Stamos name carried too much clout.

"We need to talk, Father Connelly."

Mike glanced at the man who had stopped beside him. "Hello, Giorgio. Aren't you going to introduce me to our host?"

Giorgio put his hand on Mike's elbow and steered him deeper into the ship. "Don't get smart. The boss doesn't want us taking any chances on this."

Mike maintained his Father Connelly expression. This was his first time working with Giorgio Tzekas. He was the first officer of the ship, which would have been a well-paid position for someone who didn't have expensive habits. Mike didn't have much confidence in him, but the boss had brought him in, so Mike didn't have any choice. "I wouldn't mind an introduction to those Stamos daughters," Mike said. "They'd look good even if they weren't loaded."

Giorgio snickered at that. It appeared Mike had found some common ground with his accomplice. "They were only here for the launch," Giorgio said. "The ship's named after their mother. But except for the granddaughter, none of the Stamos family is on this sailing."

That was just as well, Mike decided. For what they were planning, they didn't want any extra scrutiny.

MARINA COULD HEAR the music from the pier below as she hurried along the deck. The dance troupe had left the stage and was weaving through the crowd, encouraging the on-lookers to join them. Everyone seemed determined to enjoy themselves on this cruise, even before it started.

Stefan would love the music, Marina thought. He'd first responded to his mother's singing when he'd been an infant, and no wonder—Olena could sing like a lark. Oh, how their home had rung with music when Olena would sing to Borya's balalaika.

Marina clamped her teeth together to keep her chin from trembling. She'd never been good at tempering her emotions, but she couldn't remember being on the verge of tears this often. And why now, when she was so close to seeing her nephew? She should be happy.

Yet the same thing had happened after she'd left home. Often she would spend a year at a stretch in Moscow, thriving on her independence and on the challenge of her work, but the mere thought of being with her family again would make her crumble. Whenever she'd returned to Murmansk for a visit, her tears would start before the train had arrived at the station.

She shaded her eyes and scanned the crowd of people at the railing that ran along the outside of the deck. *Alexandra's Dream* was only a midsize cruise ship, yet there would still be over a thousand passengers. The odds of spotting Stefan were slim. It would be more logical for Marina to contact David Anderson once he got to his state-room than try to find one small boy in this crowd.

Yet how could she be logical when she might be no more than a few yards from her nephew? They had to be here. Surely the American thief wouldn't deny her nephew the chance to watch the ship leave the harbor. Stefan would be so excited to be on a vessel this size, he would be dancing with excitement. And just the thought of holding him again was making Marina's arms ache.

There, on the far side of the deck, a tall man stood alone with a child and, dear God, was that a flash of blond hair?

Marina's pulse tripped. She couldn't see the boy's face from here. She didn't recognize his clothes, either. He seemed taller than Stefan.

Almost a year had passed since she'd seen her nephew. She'd postponed her Milan showing last July so that she could go home for his fourth birthday. Of course, he would be taller and would have different clothes by now. Yet there was something about the way the boy stood that seemed familiar. That had to be Stefan. She could *feel* it.

A family with cameras and identical wide-brimmed sunhats moved in front of her, blocking her view. Marina went around them, heading to the place where she had last seen the man and boy. They were no longer there, but they hadn't gone far. She could see them moving past the deck chairs that were lined up along the curve of the bow. The man was holding the child's hand and gesturing toward the sea with his free arm.

"Stefan?" Marina called.

The boy didn't react, but the man did. His back stiffened. Keeping a firm grasp on the child's hand, he looked behind him to scan the people who strolled along the deck.

Marina had a brief impression of beige clothes, broad shoulders and a square jaw, but she didn't spare the man more than a glance. All her attention was focused on the child beside him. His hair was as straight and fine as Olena's had been and only a shade lighter than her own. It lifted in the breeze that blew across the water, fluffing like a halo in the sunshine. "Stefan!" she repeated, striding forward.

The boy turned then, and Marina's steps faltered. He had blue eyes like Olena's and a dimple in his chin like Borya's. He had the same upturned button nose she used to kiss and pretend to nibble. The familiar, adorable ears that curved out a little too far protruded between strands of his hair. He had the face of her nephew…but he had a gaze she didn't recognize.

There was no mistake: this was Stefan. Yet where was the little boy who used to laugh and launch himself into her arms as soon as he saw her? He wasn't moving toward her, nor was he smiling. Instead he was sucking his thumb, a habit she thought he'd given up at three, except when he had stayed up too late or was upset about something.

She choked back a sob. The loss she'd felt these past nine months was nothing compared with what Stefan must have gone through to have changed this much. She hadn't found him a moment too soon. She closed the remaining distance between them at a run, dropped to her knees and held out her arms. "Stefochka, my heart," she cried, automatically using Russian. "I've missed you so much."

He didn't reply. His lips began to tremble around his thumb.

The man, who had to be Anderson, acted smoothly, placing himself between her and Stefan before she could touch him. "It's okay, son," he said in English. He kept his voice low and steady, his tone pleasant. "She's mixed-up, that's all. Ma'am? Please, move away."

Marina shoved her hair out of her eyes and braced one hand on the deck so she could look at her nephew past the barrier of the American's legs. It had been almost a year, but he couldn't have forgotten her already, could he? "Stefan, darling," she said, still speaking in Russian. "I'm sorry I couldn't find you for so long, but I'm here now and—"

"Ma'am, for my son's sake, I don't want to make a scene, so I'd like you to leave on your own."

She brushed off his request with a flick of her fingers. David Anderson sounded as passionless as her lawyer. Couldn't he see how upset Stefan was? And how dare he call Stefan *his* son? The American couldn't even speak her nephew's native tongue.

Yet this wasn't the time to take issue with the words or the language he used. All that mattered was Stefan. His face was flushing. He looked as if he was about to break into tears. She smiled and tried again. "Stefan, sweetie, I—"

Before Marina could finish her plea, Anderson caught her wrist and raised her to her feet. She was too surprised to resist at first. She wasn't a small woman, so she wasn't accustomed to being hauled around by anyone, yet this man had pulled her up effortlessly with only one arm. "I don't know what your problem is or how you know my son's name," he said. His tone was still pleasant, although his voice had dropped. Keeping a grip on Stefan with his other hand, he leaned his head toward Marina so he could speak next to her ear. "But whatever you're saying is upsetting my child. Get away from us. Now."

Marina switched to English. "I have more right to call this child mine than you do, as my lawyer should have already informed you."

"What?"

"I'm Marina Artamova."

"Who?"

"Stefan's aunt."

Anderson's fingers tightened on her wrist. "What are you doing here? How did you get on board?"

"I'm taking a cruise vacation, just like you."

He was silent for a moment, then stepped close enough for his breath to stir her hair. "I don't care if you're the Princess Anastasia coming back from the dead to claim the Russian throne," he said. "You had no right to shock Stefan this way. Can't you see that you're making him cry?"

Marina arched backward so she could better see her nephew past the bulk of Anderson's body. Stefan's tiny hand was engulfed by the American's, but he didn't appear to be trying to pull away. He was leaning against the man's leg and watching her solemnly. Tears brimmed on his lower eyelids. His cheeks pumped hard as he worked at his thumb.

She didn't want to believe her impulsive greeting had been the cause of his distress. Yet what did she know about children? Olena had been the maternal one, not her, as she had pointed out whenever Marina had given Stefan a toy that wasn't safe, or had brought him an outfit that wasn't practical. Marina had always meant well, but—

"I'll give you three seconds to back off," Anderson said. "Then I'm going to call the ship's security and have them escort you away."

On top of all the emotions that were churning inside her, his threat hit Marina like a slap. *He* would dare to call security on *her?* He was the criminal, taking advantage of a bureaucrat's error to steal her nephew from his only remaining family. She was Stefan's aunt. Regardless of the mistakes she might make, no one loved this boy more than her.

She tore her gaze from Stefan and glared at Anderson. She had to tip back her head to do it, since he was half a head taller than her in spite of the heels she wore.

He met her scowl with an expression that was as blandly pleasant as the tone of voice he'd been using. On the surface, that is. But there was nothing bland about his features. His square jaw, hawk nose and deeply lined cheeks would have suited a cowboy from America's legendary Wild West. His eyes were the color of amber and appeared harder than the gemstone they resembled. A network of tiny wrinkles spread from their corners, as if he'd stared across one too many lone prairie.

Marina knew he wasn't a cowboy. Rudolph had told her that David Anderson was an ordinary schoolteacher from Vermont. Yet apart from the conservative golf shirt and tailored slacks this man wore, he didn't appear to fit the part of any schoolteacher Marina could imagine. He didn't seem like the type of person who would want to adopt a child, either. He looked too tough and self-contained.

Anderson shifted his grip from her wrist to her elbow, as if he was preparing to propel her across the deck. "Two seconds," he said pleasantly.

She glanced at Stefan. He was watching them intently. The tip of his thumb gleamed wetly where it rested on his lower lip. At least he was no longer sucking it. She drew in a deep breath in an effort to calm herself. It wasn't in her nature to retreat, but for Stefan's sake she had to take a stab at diplomacy.

"Mr. Anderson," she said. "My emotions have made me forget myself. Please forgive me. This isn't how I meant to approach you, but it has been close to a year since I saw my nephew and I was overcome. I love him dearly and would never want to upset him."

"That's good."

"Just as I'm sure you wouldn't want to upset him further by causing his aunt to be taken away by force."

"I wasn't bluffing, Miss Artamova. I will do whatever is necessary for the good of my son."

Her skin began to heat where Anderson was holding her elbow, reminding her of the strength he'd demonstrated earlier. She returned her gaze to his and lifted her chin. "Then in that case," she said, "you won't object to discussing the situation we find ourselves in."

"A situation you created." A muscle twitched in the hollow of his cheek. "Why are you really here, Miss Artamova? And don't tell me you're taking a vacation."

"Obviously, I'm here to see my nephew and to talk to you."

"Why?" he repeated.

"Because I don't want to have our discussion in a courtroom."

"Neither do I." He released her arm. "But this is hardly the right time or place to arrange a visitation schedule."

"It's not visitation I wish to discuss, Mr. Anderson, it's custody."

Although he didn't move so much as a muscle, Marina had to fight the urge to step back. The mild expression he'd managed to maintain was slipping, she realized. The lines on his face seemed deeper, his eyes harder. Had she been wrong to think the man was passionless? Yet when he finally spoke, his voice was as steady as before. "Whatever we discuss will be done through proper channels. My lawyer's name is Harold Rothsburger. Have your lawyer contact him. He's in the Burlington, Vermont, phone book."

Afterward, Marina was never sure whether she would have actually accepted his dismissal and left of her own volition then or not. She realized she should have, no matter how much it would have broken her heart to have walked away from Stefan now that she'd finally found him. She'd made a mess of her opening foray, so the smart move would be a strategic retreat. At least until the ship had left the harbor. Once they were at sea, Anderson couldn't avoid her indefinitely.

But when she tried to take a step back, she found that she was still being held in place. She glanced down.

With one hand firmly in his adoptive father's grasp, Stefan had reached out with the other and was clutching a fold of Marina's skirt. A circle of dampness darkened the silk near his thumb. He was hanging on so tightly, his knuckles were white. "*'Tyo Nina?*"

It was what he'd called her when he'd been a baby. For an instant, time collapsed and she felt as if she were back on the train platform at the Murmansk station and was about to step into the arms of her family.

But the rest of her family was gone. Only this precious little boy remained.

It was no longer any use to try to hold back her tears. They flowed freely down her cheeks as she laid her hand over Stefan's. "*Da,* Stefanichka. It's Aunt Nina."

He grabbed her fingers hard, as if he were afraid she would pull her hand away.

Marina licked a tear from the corner of her mouth and leaned down to plant a noisy kiss on her nephew's fingers.

Diplomacy was overrated.

Retreat had never worked for her, anyway.

And unless David Anderson was willing to pick her up and throw her overboard in front of a shipload of witnesses, there was no way he was going to keep her from this child now.

CHAPTER TWO

DAVID RESTED HIS hand on Stefan's back, letting it ride the soft rise and fall of his breathing as he sank deeper into sleep. Dressed in his bright red Spider-Man pajamas, the little boy could have passed for an ordinary five-year-old. The wariness had dropped from his face, leaving him with the peaceful innocence that should have been his all along.

It was an awesome responsibility, to be entrusted with the welfare of a child. David had thought he was prepared for parenthood—he'd been eager for it—yet he hadn't expected his feelings to deepen so fast. Did every father feel this protective? Maybe caring for a defenseless child, keeping him safe, was the true purpose of a man's strength.

"Good night, son," David whispered, tucking the coverlet over Stefan's shoulders. "Sweet dreams."

Stefan's thumb twitched on the pillow. He gave a shuddering sigh, then resumed his even breathing.

David stood up from the twin bed, taking care not to jar the mattress. The bedroom he'd prepared for Stefan at home was full of primary colors, with round-edged, durable maple furniture and an easily washable corduroy bedspread. The shelves were crammed with every book and toy imaginable, a large percentage of them gifts from his family and his students. It was a place where a boy could relax and be a boy. It bore no resemblance to this elegant, seashell-pink-and-white stateroom.

Still, the clean lines and subdued colors of this room were peaceful, and peace was what Stefan needed right now. Although he hadn't spoken much, his actions and body language had clearly shown his excitement. Everything about the ship thrilled him, even the mandatory lifeboat drill before they'd left the harbor. By the time *Alexandra's Dream* had started to move, Stefan had sported the telltale flushed-cheek, glassy-eyed look of an overtired child.

"Is he asleep?"

Marina's rich, accented voice sliced through the calm. David gritted his teeth. She was another reason Stefan had become overtired. The child already had enough of an emotional adjustment to handle without having a surprise appearance by his long-lost aunt thrown into the mix.

Marina Artamova had a hell of a lot of nerve, booking passage on this cruise in order to ambush them. And it had been an effective strategy. Once Stefan had recognized his aunt, it would have upset him more if David had tried to separate them. She'd taken full advantage of that and had stuck to them like glue until David had given her the number of his stateroom and promised to talk to her in private after Stefan had gone to sleep. Even so, she had shown up early.

What kind of woman would use a child's feelings for her as a means to get her way? That rankled David. Stefan was vulnerable and hungry for affection; he could all too easily be hurt if Marina's apparent devotion turned out to be more show than substance.

Placing his finger to his lips, he moved past the other bed and walked to the stateroom's small balcony, where he'd asked her to wait. "Stefan settled down fast," he said once he was outside. He focused on his hands, concentrating on sliding the glass door closed soundlessly in spite of the sudden urge he felt to slam something. "He was exhausted."

"Will he be all right in there alone?"

He shifted his focus to look past the streaks of sunset that were reflected on the glass. Dusk had darkened the room, so David had left the light in the bathroom on and the door partly ajar. He could see the bed—Stefan was still curled on his side, facing the wall. "I'm only a few steps away."

"If he wakes up by himself and gets frightened—"

"I appreciate your concern, Miss Artamova," he said, turning to face her. "But I know how to handle children. If my son needs me, I'll go inside and comfort him."

She stood at the railing, the darkening sky and the sea providing a spectacular backdrop. People came from all over the world to enjoy the sunsets on the Mediterranean, but Marina seemed oblivious to the scenery. She didn't appear to notice the snatches of conversation and laughter that came from the neighboring balconies or the dance music that drifted from one of the decks. It was the first night of the cruise, and the other passengers were celebrating, yet Marina had her back to the rail, her arms crossed and her feet braced apart as if she were preparing for a fight.

Although she had followed his lead and kept their conversation in front of Stefan as neutral as possible, it had been obvious to David that she wasn't accustomed to restraining herself. Her next words confirmed his guess.

"*Your* son doesn't exist," she said. "You adopted a boy named Stefan Sigorsky from St. Petersburg who had no living relatives. The child who is sleeping in that room is Stefan Gorsky from Murmansk and is my nephew."

David tried to keep his frustration from showing and to think of something civil to say, but it wasn't easy. Harold had discovered the spelling error in Stefan's name when the adoption had been nearly complete. It was the reason the information on Stefan's family background had been so patchy. David could understand why Marina would believe that gave her grounds to challenge his custody.

Even if she had approached him through more conventional channels rather than choosing to sidestep their lawyers and disrupt his first trip with Stefan, he still wouldn't feel like talking to her. The bare fact was that this woman wanted to take his son away. David wasn't going to let her. As far as he was concerned, there was nothing more to discuss.

But Marina Artamova didn't appear to be the kind of woman who would be easy to silence. As a matter of fact, there wasn't anything quiet about her. She had the kind of presence that would get noticed before she spoke a word, and it wasn't due only to her height.

Taken one at a time, her features were too strong to be considered pretty—her nose was defiantly large, and her full lips weren't capable of looking dainty or sweet—yet the overall effect was striking. Her straight hair streamed behind her in a luscious fall of pale gold. Every imaginable shade of blue and green swirled through the fabric of her dress. The dress was swirling, too, shaping and re-shaping itself against her body with each puff of wind from the water. And as if that didn't attract enough attention, silver bracelets tinkled along her slender arm with the slightest gesture she made.

She didn't look like the spinster aunt he'd imagined when he'd first heard about her. Nor did she look like the type of woman who would want to take on the responsibility of a child. She was too...vivid. Passionate. A child needed order and stability. Marina didn't come close to David's idea of anyone's mother.

He folded his arms over his chest, unconsciously mirroring her stance. "My lawyer and I fought through the bureaucracy of two countries to arrange for Stefan to come home with me. The misspelled name changes nothing because all the necessary documents were corrected. He is the same child I adopted. Legally, I am his father."

"You are not a blood relative," she said. "I am."

He wished he could dispute that claim, but any doubts he might have harbored over her identity had been settled the moment he'd looked into her eyes. The family resemblance there was unmistakable—her eyes were green instead of Stefan's pale blue, but they were wide-set like his and had the same tilt at the corners. Unlike her nephew, though, Marina wasn't wary about showing her feelings. She wore her emotions as flamboyantly as her clothes.

It wasn't surprising that Stefan had been startled when she had swooped down and tried to envelope him in those yards of floating silk and hair.

"Miss Artamova," he said, "do you care about your nephew?"

"What a ridiculous question. Of course I care about him." Her bracelets tinkled as she splayed one hand over her breast. "I love him with all my heart."

He kept his gaze on her face, in spite of the way her gesture had drawn the fabric of her dress tight across her bust. She'd already manipulated him once. She could be trying to use that gesture as a deliberate attempt to distract him. "Then think about him instead of yourself. Your presence here will only end up hurting Stefan."

"How can you say that? You saw for yourself how much he wanted me to stay with him. He was happy to see me…eventually," she added.

"You're confusing him. The more time you spend with him, the worse he will feel when you have to say goodbye at the end of the cruise."

She dropped her hand and stepped away from the railing. "The goodbye won't be forever. My lawyer is presenting a petition to reverse your adoption."

No! he wanted to shout. Stefan was *his* child. "Your claim was too late."

"Too late to stop this mistake, but not too late to correct it. Check with your Mr. Rothsburger if you don't trust my word."

Oh, he planned to verify everything with Harold as soon as possible. He knew better than to trust the word of any woman. Ellie had claimed to want Stefan, too, but her actions had spoken louder than her words.

Parenting was a lifetime commitment. David knew all too well that not everyone was cut out for the long haul. And when they bailed out, it was the child who suffered. "Where do you live, Miss Artamova?"

She tilted her head, sending a wisp of gold hair sliding across her cheek. "I have an apartment in Moscow. What difference does that make?"

"It must be close to a thousand miles from Moscow to Murmansk. Your nephew didn't recognize you at first. I have to assume you couldn't have seen him very often."

"It's fourteen hundred kilometers, but I saw him as often as I could." She stopped abruptly. "I do not need to make excuses. Don't try to measure my devotion to my nephew by a calendar or a clock, Mr. Anderson, or you will be the one to come up short. You have known him less than two days."

"I began adoption proceedings seven months ago, yet you didn't bother to file a protest until the last minute. It makes me question how committed you are."

"Didn't *bother?*" She pushed one of the deck chairs aside and moved toward him. The balcony was narrow, so she closed the distance between them in three steps. "It wasn't lack of interest that kept me from Stefan. I was in Paris when my sister and brother-in-law died. I didn't learn about the accident until I returned home, and by that time Stefan was gone. They said he'd been transferred, but no one knew where. I searched every inch of the Murmansk orphanage anyway. Six times. I offered rewards, I tried bribes. I even tried prayer. I've lived every minute since last August with a part of my heart missing."

She lifted her hand, but instead of splaying it on her chest this time, she placed her palm gently on the glass door. She turned her face toward the room and looked at the child on the bed. "You can question my actions, Mr. Anderson, but don't ever question my love."

She was crying again, just as she had when Stefan had said her name on the deck earlier. It wasn't any delicate, ladylike sniffling. The tears flowed unchecked down her cheeks and dripped from her jaw.

She didn't appear to notice. It was as if all the combativeness she'd armed herself with in order to confront David had cracked and fallen away. She was watching Stefan, her lips trembling into a smile of naked tenderness.

A man would have to be made of stone not to be moved by that smile. Shaken, David unfolded his arms. He hadn't realized he'd reached for her until his palm was an inch from Marina's shoulder. Against all logic, he wanted to comfort her. It didn't make sense. How could he consider comforting her when she wanted to take his son away?

He drew back his arm before he could touch her.

"I've blown it, haven't I?" she asked softly. "That's what you Americans say."

"Depends what you're talking about."

She made a noise in her throat halfway between a sob and a laugh. Shaking her head, she grabbed the end of her scarf and used it to dry her face. "My lawyer warned me I could make matters worse, but I thought it would be better for Stefan if we didn't drag him through the courts. I wanted you and me to settle this between us by the end of the cruise. That's why I booked my ticket, so we could use the next ten days to discuss our predicament together." She dropped her scarf, leaned her forehead against the door and heaved a sigh. "But then I saw Stefan and I forgot all the very logical and reasonable arguments I'd prepared."

David could no longer see her mouth—her hair had swung forward to drape her cheeks. The breeze toyed with the ends of her hair the way it swirled her dress against her body, stirring the scent of apples.

The scent didn't seem exotic enough for a woman as flamboyant as Marina. Yet the simple, honest tang of apples fit perfectly with a woman who would weep as she watched a sleeping child.

David continued to study her. His instincts were gradually overriding his doubts. Unless she was the world's greatest actress, her feelings for Stefan *had* to be genuine.

That didn't mean she would make a good mother.

Regardless of Marina's protests, David was still Stefan's

legal guardian and nothing she could say would change his mind about that. The law was on his side, too. It would be within his rights to complain to the cruise staff and have them keep Marina away from him and Stefan for the rest of the voyage.

Yet it wouldn't be fair to cut Stefan off from his only living relative. Children needed all the family they could get.

And what about afterward, when he and Stefan got home? If Marina followed through with the custody suit, the case could become mired in the jurisdictional tangles of international law and take years to sort through. Stefan's fate could be in limbo until he was old enough to go to college…that is, if David had any money left to send him there after he paid his lawyer's fee.

In light of that scenario, any possibility of settling the case out of court would be worth pursuing, no matter how unconventional the method might seem. He was so obviously the right parent for Stefan, he was confident he could convince Marina of that.

Once she heard his side, they wouldn't need the courts.

"Miss Artamova," he said finally. "I would go to any lengths to avoid putting Stefan through the ordeal of a formal custody dispute. I agree with you that it would be better to work things out between us."

She rolled her forehead along the glass and peered at him through one eye. "You do?"

He nodded. "As long as you don't do or say anything to upset Stefan again, I'm willing to listen to your arguments. I'll make a copy of our daily schedule for you so we can arrange some convenient times to meet."

She straightened from the door. "Oh, thank you, Mr. Anderson."

He held up his palm to stop her. "But while I'll listen to you, you also have to be willing to hear my side."

"Of course. That's all I ask. You'll see that—" She stopped and returned her gaze to the glass door.

David heard the cry at the same moment she did. He shoved the door open and strode to Stefan's bed.

Stefan had been relaxed and sleeping on his side when David had left him, but now he'd pulled his legs to his chest and was curled into a tight ball. He was breathing fast, his eyelids rippling with the rapid movement of his eyes.

"It's okay, Stefan," David said quietly. He braced one knee on the edge of the bed and touched his shoulder gently so he wouldn't startle him. "I'm right here."

Although Stefan didn't open his eyes, David's voice appeared to soothe him. His breathing hitched, then slowed from a sprint to a jog.

"I'll always be here when you need me," David continued, skimming his palm along Stefan's arm. "You're safe now. I promise. There's nothing for you to worry about anymore." He sat on the edge of the mattress so he could reach the coverlet that Stefan had pushed aside. He tucked it around Stefan, more for its comforting weight than for its warmth, all the while speaking in the same soothing tone.

Whatever dream had disturbed Stefan's rest didn't last long. He sank back into sleep after a few minutes. The same thing had happened the night before, when they'd stayed at an Athens hotel after their flight from St. Petersburg. David was concerned, but not alarmed. Considering the recent upheavals in this child's life, a few bad dreams wouldn't be unusual.

"He can't understand you," Marina whispered. "Why is that working?"

David glanced over his shoulder to see that she'd followed him into the room. She stood in the narrow space between the beds, her hands clasped together and pressed to her midriff. In the soft glow of the light that spilled from the bathroom doorway, her resemblance to Stefan seemed stronger than before. Not so much her features as her expression. She looked…lost. Alone. Hungry for affection.

If he stretched his arm, he'd be able to touch her. Again, he had a nearly overwhelming urge to do just that.

But once more, David reminded himself who she was and why she was here. He kept his arm by his side.

"He understands what I'm feeling," he replied. "He knows I mean what I say. I'm not going to let anything—or anyone—ever hurt this child."

NIGHT HAD FALLEN six hours ago, but the section of Moscow where Ilya Fedorovich lived was far from silent. A siren echoed along the buildings of stone and brick that lined the narrow street. Rock music from the bar on the corner seeped through the crack under the windowsill along with the sour sewer smell of cooked cabbage. The couple next door was having noisy sex again, rattling the glasses in the sink as their bed slammed into the wall.

It wouldn't have occurred to Ilya that he could have afforded a better apartment. He cared nothing for his comfort. He valued the fees he earned as a testament to his success rather than a measure of riches. His work could take him anywhere, and on the rare occasions when he stayed here, this place served his need for privacy admirably.

So he ignored the noises from the street and from next door, adjusted the light over his kitchen table and held his phone to his ear. "I'm listening, Sergei."

"She left her apartment yesterday. I put her suitcases in the taxi myself."

Ilya used his free hand to take a neatly folded polishing cloth from the stack beside the bottle of gun oil. "That isn't unusual. She travels often. You said you had news for me."

"*Da.* You asked me to keep my eyes open. I did not forget."

Most of Ilya's Moscow contacts claimed to be keeping their eyes open but they had learned nothing helpful yet. "Fine. Go on."

"I suspected right away it was no ordinary business trip. She had enough luggage to fill the taxi."

He ran the cloth over the chromed barrel of the 9 mm Makarov that lay on the felt pad in the center of the table. "Anything else?"

"I didn't know where she went until her secretary and her lawyer came to the building this evening to get some contracts she'd forgotten to return to the office. I overheard them talking. They were very displeased with how quickly she had left. She canceled all her appointments and went on a Mediterranean cruise."

"Sergei, this still is no use to me. I'm not interested in her holiday plans."

"But that's why I called. I've been doorman at the Black Eagle Arms for seven years, and the only holidays she took were when she went home to Murmansk."

Ilya brought the pistol barrel near his nose. He allowed himself a moment to indulge in the scent of warm gun oil, then tilted the weapon toward the light and inspected the metal for any trace of lint. "Yes. I know. Perhaps she wanted a milder climate."

"*Nyet,* that wasn't why she went on the cruise." Sergei

paused and dropped his voice. "Her secretary said she was going to see her nephew."

His fingers spasmed around the phone. He would tighten them around Sergei's neck if this news was yet another false lead. "Did you say 'nephew'?"

"That's what I heard them say. It must be true. It's probably why she was excited when she left. That's how she used to be before she went on a trip to Murmansk. She must have found that boy you were looking for."

"Excellent. You were right to call me."

Sergei cleared his throat. "She gave me a thousand ruble tip when she left."

"I will give you ten thousand if you can tell me what port she was departing from."

"I'm sorry, I can't. She told the taxi to go to the airport, that's all."

"That's worthless. She could have flown anywhere from Stockholm to Istanbul."

"I know. I'm sorry. Her secretary complained about that to the lawyer. He told her they had to fax the contracts they picked up at the apartment straight to the ship."

Ilya's nostrils flared like those of a predator finally getting within sensing distance of its prey. "The ship? Did they mention its name?"

"*Da!* It's *Alexandra's Dream.*"

The couple next door completed their business with a thump and a pair of hoarse screams. A horn blared from the street. Somewhere in the distance a dog began to bark. Ilya heard none of it over the quick throb of his pulse. "Well done, Sergei."

"Thank you, Colonel!"

He terminated the call and placed the phone on the

table, savoring the sound of his rank as much as he'd savored the smell of his gun. Few people addressed him as Colonel anymore, but Sergei had served in his unit and would remember. Ilya didn't delude himself by thinking the courtesy was anything more than an attempt to curry favor, though.

The world had changed since the glory days of the Soviet Army. Loyalty had had meaning then. A soldier had honor and dignity. Sergei could have no pride left, if he was content to open doors and live off the charity of the wealthy *novye russkie*.

Still, he had proved himself useful. Sergei's lack of honor was going to allow Ilya to fulfill his duty.

Because while the world had changed, Ilya hadn't. His word was his bond. From the time he'd first understood his purpose in life, he'd built his reputation on a perfect record. His medals attested to that. He moved his gaze to the framed collection that hung above the table. The army had decorated him and promoted him to the rank of colonel in recognition of his skill. He worked for the highest bidder now, and was paid well for exercising his craft, yet the work was the same.

He looked at the weapon in his hand. Work? No, dealing out death was more than a profession to Ilya, it was a calling. He stroked his index finger along the gun barrel, relishing the slide of the slick metal under his skin. He was good at what he did. The best. When he took a contract, he didn't stop until it was complete.

Killing the fisherman and his family should have presented little challenge. The man had been a nobody who'd made the fatal mistake of defying the local *Mafiya*. The three deaths would have served as an example to others, and as always, Ilya had intended to show no mercy when he dealt out the punishment. The hit had started well—it had been pathetically easy to knock the Gorsky car off the road. There had been no witnesses, and there should have been no survivors. Borya Gorsky was dead. So was his wife.

But their child had lived. He had escaped. He'd been taken to an orphanage and then had disappeared without a trace, defying every attempt Ilya had made to track him down.

Until now.

Ilya's teeth closed hard on the ridge of scar tissue that extended through his cheek. Instantly his mouth filled with the familiar, copper-sweet taste of warm blood. He closed his eyes and rubbed the tip of the gun against the line on the outside, trying to soothe the ache, but he knew only one thing would grant him relief when the old wound began to throb.

He had to finish the job.

And thanks to Marina Artamova's determination to find her nephew, now he could.

CHAPTER THREE

"YES, THEY'RE RIGHT over there, Mrs. Anderson."

Marina looked past an array of glass-fronted wooden bookshelves and plush armchairs to the corner the librarian had indicated. David and Stefan were seated on an over-stuffed sofa near the room's far wall. Bathed in the soft glow from one of the pot lights in the library's ceiling, they could have been posing for an artist's portrait. They looked relaxed and natural, the picture of togetherness, snuggled close beside each other as Stefan tipped his head toward the book that David held on his lap.

The contrast between the broad-shouldered, dark-haired man and the slight blond boy was more than visually appealing, it was touching. They looked almost as sweet as they had the night before when David had sat on Stefan's bed to comfort him.

Marina hadn't been able to get that image out of her mind. In particular, she kept remembering how David's large hand had rested so gently on the whimsically patterned red pajamas that had covered Stefan's back. In spite of her concern over her nephew, she'd been far too conscious of how strong and very male David had looked against the pink shadows of that stateroom.

She wasn't comfortable with the fact that she was

thinking about David at all. It didn't make sense. Aside from their interest in Stefan, they had nothing in common. He was an American schoolteacher from Vermont who drew up schedules—schedules!—for his day with a five-year-old. That's how she'd known they would be in the ship's library; it had been item number two for today, right after breakfast and before a visit to the observation deck.

Furthermore, David dressed in clothes that would bore a corpse. Although it did show off the breadth of his shoulders, his shirt was unremarkable, department-store cotton, and his pants appeared to be the same off-the-rack beige ones he'd worn yesterday. What's more, she could count on one hand the number of times she'd seen any emotion on his face. He appeared determined to wall up his feelings behind dry words and bland smiles. What kind of father was that for a lively boy like Stefan?

So she had no business wondering whether the man who had held her wrist as boldly as a cowboy the day before would also be able to caress a woman as gently as he touched a child. David Anderson was her adversary. Thinking of him in any capacity other than that was preposterous.

Marina swallowed a sigh. It had been an intense few days. Actually it had been an intense several months. She'd been stressed and emotionally exhausted. Noticing that a man looked like, well, a *man* was nothing to dwell on. She was, after all, a woman.

"Your son is adorable," the librarian said.

The comment brought a pang to Marina's heart. She glanced at the librarian's name tag. "He's my nephew, not my son, Miss Bennett. And Mr. Anderson is not my husband."

"Oh, I'm sorry. You looked so much like your nephew I just assumed he was yours." Ariana Bennett smiled shyly, fiddling with the stack of books she held in her arms. She was almost the same height as Marina, only she had the slim build of a swimmer. Dark brown hair fell in waves to her shoulders in a sensual contrast to her studious demeanor. "And I still think he's adorable. You don't often see children that quiet and well-behaved. He must love books as much as I do."

Marina could make no response to that. For one thing, she hadn't known that Stefan liked books. For another, he'd seldom been so quiet whenever she had gone to visit. He used to squeal and run around the house laughing with her until he broke something or threw up. That always used to annoy Olena, who would sigh and tell them both to behave.

God, what she wouldn't give to hear her sister scold them again. Or to see that tiny apartment the Gorsky family had filled with love…

At the first warning prickle behind her eyes she tamped down the memories and started across the room. She'd had enough of the waterworks the day before. It was time to get down to the business she'd come for, which meant convincing David Anderson that Stefan belonged with her.

She reached the sofa where they sat and smiled a greeting at Stefan. "Good morning, Stevovochik."

Her nephew jerked his head up immediately. He parted his lips as if he were about to greet her, then glanced at David. "*'Tyo Nina?'*"

David leaned his head toward Stefan and spoke in a stage whisper. "Aunt Marina."

"Aunt," Stefan repeated carefully. His eyes sparkled as he looked at her. "Aunt Nina."

The sound of English coming from Stefan's lips jarred her. She'd thought he didn't understand it. That had been the first point she'd planned to make in her favor today: she could speak Stefan's language but David couldn't. Any reasonable person would see that would make her the better choice for a parent.

"We're having an English lesson," David said.

She glanced at the book that lay open across his thighs. It was a children's picture book. She twisted her neck to focus on the illustration and saw it was a huge letter *B* that was covered with colorful images.

"He's a fast learner," David said. He pointed to the bottom of the page. "What's that, Stefan?"

As Stefan leaned against David's arm to look, Marina squeezed onto the sofa beside Stefan. A black-and-red tugboat rode on the water that filled the bottom loop of the *B*. "Boat," Stefan said, jabbing his small finger against the page next to David's. "Boat."

"And this?" David asked, flipping the edges of the pages with his thumb.

"Book." Stefan slid his finger to the top of the *B* where an open book was propped against a baseball bat. "Book. Bat."

"Right." David tapped his fingertips against his own chest. "And me?"

"Dad!"

David reached in front of Stefan to tap Marina's shoulder. "What about her? Do you remember?"

"Aunt Nina!" Stefan smiled and bounced on the cushion, obviously enjoying the game.

Except his bouncing knocked David's fingertips from Marina's shoulder to her breast. She gasped as his palm grazed her nipple. "Mr. Anderson!"

David snatched his arm away as if he'd been scalded. His elbow caught the edge of the picture book and knocked it to the floor. "Excuse me," he murmured, leaning over to retrieve the book.

Marina resisted the urge to rub the place where he'd touched her. The contact had been momentary, hardly more than a slight pressure against the front of her blouse, barely perceptible through the layers of lace and linen that had separated her skin from his.

Yet her skin tingled. And her nipple was starting to tighten.

She gritted her teeth and tried to ignore it. She must be more stressed than she'd thought.

At her silence, Stefan looked from her to David, his smile wavering.

"You did great, son," David said cheerfully, ruffling Stefan's hair. "Didn't he, Marina?"

"You mean, the English lesson?" she asked.

He met her gaze over Stefan's head. "Of course that's what I meant," he replied. He placed the book in Stefan's hands, pointed to it and then at a low table near one of the bookcases. Several more colorful picture books lay on the table. "Put the book with the others," he said slowly. "Over there."

Stefan nodded, clutched the book to his chest and slid from the sofa. He headed straight for the table, apparently understanding the instruction perfectly.

"Children can pick up languages at an amazing pace," David said, watching Stefan's progress across the floor. "He'll be fluent in no time."

Marina remembered the point she'd wanted to make. "He wouldn't need to learn English if he stayed in Russia with me."

"Then why did you learn it?"

"When I first moved to Moscow, my landlord had a Canadian wife who became my friend. I asked her to teach me English, because I thought it would give me an advantage when dealing with foreigners."

"Yes, English is considered the universal language in much of the world."

"That's true. Much of my business is done in English."

"So being able to speak it would be an advantage for anyone, including Stefan. Isn't it fortunate that I happen to be a teacher?"

This wasn't going the way she'd hoped. He was twisting the point she'd tried to make to his advantage. "Is that why you are so fond of schedules, because you're a teacher?"

"It's good to plan ahead, especially when dealing with children. Routines give them stability." He made a thumbs-up sign to Stefan as the boy placed the book on the table with the others. "By the way, Marina, what kind of work do you do?"

"I design clothes."

"I see."

"What does that mean?"

"You seem like a creative person. Very, ah, unconventional."

"Was that an insult?"

"Absolutely not. I admire talent." He gave her outfit a brief perusal. His gaze lingered on her neckline for an instant before he glanced back at Stefan. "Is that one of your creations? It's very colorful."

She smoothed her hand over a wrinkle in her skirt. The aquamarine linen was a few shades darker than the cropped blouse that went with it. The outfit was actually more subdued than much of her wardrobe. She liked the design because it was cut on the bias and didn't restrict her movements despite the firm fabric. Tiny gold buttons in the shape of conch shells accented both pieces. She hadn't realized before how long they would take to fasten, though—by the time she'd reached the ones at her neck she'd lost patience and left most of them undone.

"Thank you," she said. "Color is one of the trademarks of the Artamova label." She remembered another point she'd wanted to make. "Helping women look beautiful has been very profitable. I have earned an absurd amount of money for my designs, more than enough to raise Stefan properly. He'll want for nothing."

"It sounds as if you have a demanding career. You must work long hours."

She shrugged. "It is difficult to schedule creativity."

"You mentioned you were in Paris last year. Do you travel often?"

"Yes, I attend the major fashion shows and I frequently travel for business since I prefer to do my negotiations face-to-face."

"Face-to-face," he repeated. "As you're doing with me."

"Exactly."

"With a schedule as busy as yours, you wouldn't be able to spend much time at home."

She narrowed her eyes. She realized where this could lead and didn't want him to twist another point in his favor. "Whatever the demands of my career, my first priority would be Stefan's welfare. Isn't it fortunate that I happen to have the wealth to ensure it?"

Aside from a slight tightening around his jaw, David gave no response. He rose to his feet as Stefan returned. "Good job, son," he said, taking Stefan's hand. "We're going to the observation deck now, Marina. You're free to join us if you like."

Marina wasn't sure whether or not she'd scored a point in that exchange, but she was far from discouraged. There was more than a week left; she was just getting started. She stood and took Stefan's other hand. "Of course, the observation deck. Item three."

Stefan seemed happy to walk between them as they moved toward the library exit. A crowd was gathering near a semicircle of padded benches on the far side of the room. Marina recognized the portly, gray-haired man at the front of the group: it was the priest she had run into when she'd first come on board yesterday. He was talking with Miss Bennett, the librarian, while he set up a display of old pottery.

Marina had read about Father Connelly in the ship's newsletter, which she'd found in her stateroom. He would be giving a series of lectures about antiquities during the cruise, a fitting topic since many of the ports where the ship would be stopping were near historic archaeological sites. Today the ship was moored at Katakolon, a harbor that was only a short drive from the site of the first Olympic games. A tour of the Olympia ruins was item number four on David's schedule.

When she'd booked her ticket on this cruise, though, Marina had paid no attention to the activities the ship offered or its scheduled ports of call. They could have been on an icebreaker in the Arctic for all she cared. Simply walking beside Stefan, feeling his soft, little-boy fingers clasped in hers, was worth more to her than all the treasures of the ancient world.

To her dismay, she felt her eyes heat yet again. She blinked hard and focused on her surroundings. They had moved into the airy, plant-filled corridor that ran through the center of the deck and were heading for one of the elevators. Marina was still trying to grasp the size of the ship—it was more of a combination mall and hotel than a boat. "Mr. Anderson," she began.

"My students call me 'Mr. Anderson.' I'd like you to call me David."

"Why?"

"It seems friendlier."

"We are not friends."

He paused when they reached the elevator. Without letting go of Stefan, he leaned over to bring his head close to hers, just as he had during their first meeting the day before. "We may be on opposite sides, Marina," he said softly, "but we have the same goal. We both want Stefan to be happy."

"Yes, we do."

"He is very sensitive to everything around him right now," he said, lowering his voice still further. "If you can't find a way to smile and use a pleasant tone when you speak to me around him, he's going to become nervous. He'll think he did something wrong."

She could feel his breath stirring her hair again. That, plus his hushed voice, made his words seem oddly intimate. Or was he doing that deliberately to distract her? "We are not friends," she repeated, for her benefit as much as his. "We are opponents."

"Yes, we've established that. But for Stefan's sake, let's pretend we're getting along."

"I dislike pretense. I am open with my feelings."

"Really? I never would have guessed."

She hesitated. Was that a hint of humor in his eyes? They truly were an astounding shade of amber. With a color like that, perhaps it wasn't so much of a crime for him to dress in beige. "Mr. Anderson…"

"David."

"Fine. David."

"Smile."

She bared her teeth.

"Much better," he said, straightening. He pressed the button for the elevator. "While we're on the topic of names, Marina, do you mind if I ask you a question?"

"Go ahead...David," she added pointedly.

"Why do you call Stefan so many different names?"

"Do I?"

"You've used several. Stefochka. Stevovo...something."

Her smile became genuine as she returned her gaze to her nephew. "Russian is a flexible language. It lets me play with Stefan's name."

"Like Nina?"

"That was different. When Stefan was very young, he had trouble saying *Tyotya Marina* so he shortened it himself. Right, Stevovochikdya?"

Stefan smiled at the sound of the elaborate diminutive.

Encouraged by his smile, Marina swung Stefan's hand back and forth. She looked around them and spotted a glass-fronted café across the corridor from the elevator. At that moment a waitress was putting a silver tray filled with tiny, decadent-looking desserts on a stand in the front window. Appropriately the name on the sign over the door was Temptations. "I smell chocolate," Marina said. "Time for a snack."

"Perhaps later," David said, glancing at his watch. "We only finished breakfast an hour ago."

"Pah." She flicked her fingers at his protest. "Children need more than just schedules. They need fun. Stefan loves chocolate. I always used to bring him bags full of it when I visited." She closed her eyes and sniffed dramatically, then winked at her nephew. *"Shakalat?"*

Stefan bounced on his toes, his smile widening. *"Shakalat."*

"The English is almost the same," she said, pointing to a cluster of rich, dark brown chocolates shaped like starfish. *"Shakalat.* Chocolate."

"Cho-co-late," Stefan repeated. He looked at David eagerly, as if waiting for his approval of another new word.

The elevator arrived with a subdued chime and the doors slid open. David ignored it. The lines at the corners of his eyes deepened, the angle of his jaw softened and his lips relaxed into one of his surprisingly tender smiles. "Well, maybe just one."

Marina knew this was another image that would likely stick in her mind. When a man didn't show emotion often, it made all the more impact when he did.

"One?" she exclaimed. "How can anyone have only one chocolate? That is like having only one strawberry, a complete impossibility. It is like stopping after only one kiss."

David was still smiling when he looked at her mouth. It was a passing glance, over as quickly as it began, as brief as the accidental contact earlier of his palm against her breast. He hadn't even touched her this time…yet her lips tingled as if he had.

MIKE O'CONNOR CALLED up the most benevolent expression in his repertoire as he finished his spiel and opened the floor to questions. So far, the charade was holding up well. The turnout for his first lecture had been good. In spite of the tours offered at each port of call, many people wanted to be entertained on the ship. It would be more entertaining to Mike if so much of the audience wasn't of the blue-rinse hair variety, though.

Still, it figured: why shouldn't antiques be interested in antiquities?

"Father Connelly, all of your pieces look wonderful. How can you tell the difference between a reproduction and the real thing?"

Mike maintained his expression, even though that question struck a little too close for comfort. "Why, you tell the difference by the price, of course. If you can afford it, it likely isn't real." He picked up a copy of an Etruscan funeral urn. "Take this piece, for example. No humble man of the cloth would be able to pursue a hobby such as mine if he had to buy an original one of these."

There was a polite scattering of laughter. Mike thought he'd deflected the question well, until a man with a white beard piped up from the back row. "How much would the real thing be worth, Father Connelly?"

"Ah, that would depend on many factors," Mike hedged, returning the urn to the display table. Although he was no more superstitious than most actors, he didn't want to discuss dollars and cents or people might get a little *too* interested in his "hobby." "The main factors in determining the worth of an item would be its age, its condition and how rare it might be."

"What if someone digs up one of those pots in their backyard?" the same man asked. "Does it go to a museum, or is it finder's keepers?"

Mike rubbed his chin as if considering his reply. He had a good nose for cops—a survival trait in his business—and he could usually spot one a mile away. No one in this audience, including the man with the beard, was stirring his suspicions, though, so the question had to be another innocent one.

Turning up the Irish charm another notch, Mike shook his head mournfully. "Ah, you're asking a question about something that is sure to tempt a saint." He waited for the laughter to subside, then picked up a replica amphora from the third century B.C. "Fragments of common-use items like this amphora are uncovered at construction sites in cities like Rome on a regular basis. It's the responsibility of the city's archaeology department to document and assess those finds, but who can put a price on history?" He turned the piece in his hands, then placed it back on the table and gave it a loving pat. "I believe the true value of any archaeological artifact is the sense of connection it gives us to the past."

Several people nodded and smiled at that. Mike noticed the librarian was one of them.

Ariana Bennett was an anomaly in this blue-rinse crowd. She was an attractive brunette, somewhere in her early thirties, although she leaned a little too much toward the scholarly side for Mike's taste. Worse, she'd displayed an unexpected classical expertise when she'd helped him unpack his collection earlier, which meant he had to stay on his toes. He'd started boning up on his knowledge of antiquities as soon as he'd landed the guest lecturer's spot. He didn't want some bookworm of a librarian to blow his cover.

Yet in his own way, Mike truly was an expert in the field of antiquities. After all, he'd been smuggling them for more than fifteen years.

DAVID RUBBED A TOWEL over his hair to finish drying it as he left the bathroom, his gaze automatically going to Stefan's bed. Once he assured himself the boy was still sleeping peacefully, he positioned a chair in front of the TV and switched to the information program. Like all the state-rooms on *Alexandra's Dream,* this one came with access to the ship's services through the TV and an on-ship e-mail address, which allowed David to make reservations from his cabin. He scrolled through the excursions that were available for tomorrow's stop in Dubrovnik, looking for one that would be long enough to be interesting but short enough to hold Stefan's attention.

The selection was varied, ranging from an inexpensive bus ride to the scenic lookout over the harbor to private chartered boat trips to the nearby islands. David glanced at the cost of one boat trip, gave a soundless whistle and scrolled past. While he wanted to make sure Stefan got the most out of this trip, he couldn't afford to splurge on a teacher's salary. He was fortunate that his youngest sister, Keisha, ran a travel agency in Burlington and had obtained the tickets for this cruise at a deep discount.

Of course, cost wouldn't be a consideration for someone as wealthy as Marina.

She hadn't given him any specifics when she'd told him she was paid an absurd amount of money for her work, but David's lawyer had filled in the blanks. In fact, according to the message from Harold Rothsburger that David had found when he'd stopped by the ship's communications center to check his personal e-mail, Marina was much more than a designer. She'd started out that way, but now she owned a clothing store in Moscow that was expanding throughout Europe. Women from Budapest to Paris were snapping up the colorful, ultrafeminine clothes that were sold under the Artamova label. She might be emotional and impulsive, but she was also an extremely smart businesswoman.

She could definitely provide the very best care for any child she raised.

And if David couldn't convince her to settle their custody dispute out of court, she could afford to out-lawyer and outlast him. He *had* to make her change her mind.

He squeezed his jaw between his thumb and fingers as he remembered the rest of Harold's message. Marina's lawyer had indeed filed suit to reverse Stefan's adoption. It had been done in St. Petersburg, because that was where the orphanage that had finalized the adoption was located, so it was going to take a while to sort through the jurisdictional issues.

It wasn't much of a reprieve, but it did confirm what David had already thought: Stefan was still legally his son.

David hadn't yet told his family about the complication of Marina. They had sent e-mail messages, too. The one from Blanche, his older sister, had been filled with good wishes mixed with parenting tips. Like their own mother, Blanche was a stay-at-home mom, devoting herself full-time to raising her five children. Her middle boy was Stefan's age, and according to Blanche he was eagerly awaiting the arrival of his new Russian cousin.

So were the rest of Stefan's new cousins, uncles and aunts, and especially his new grandparents. The Andersons were a large and welcoming family. Once Stefan got home, there would be no shortage of playmates for him. No shortage of potential babysitters, either. When David's students had learned why he was taking this leave of absence, half of them had started lining up for the chance to babysit his new son.

He felt a jab of guilt as he remembered how he'd tried to use Marina's career as a point against her. He wasn't about to quit his own career, so he wouldn't be a full-time parent to Stefan, either. He'd need to arrange child care the same as she would.

Yet when he'd begun the adoption process, he'd thought that Stefan would have a full-time mother.

Ellie had talked about having children from the time David had married her. She used to subscribe to parenting magazines, and couldn't pass through a department store without visiting the nursery section. He'd shared the same dream. He'd hoped to create the kind of loving home with Ellie that he'd known with the Andersons.

Her failure to conceive hadn't been the only reason their marriage had become strained. If the foundation of their relationship had been solid, they would have been able to weather any problem. He realized that now. Yet at the time, David had hoped adopting a child would turn things around. For a while, their excitement over Stefan had seemed to bring them closer together.

That's why the affair she'd confessed to had hit David so hard. He'd felt duped. Used. Yet Ellie had felt no remorse over her betrayal. She'd turned it around by blaming her unfaithfulness on him.

You never loved me, David. You're too damaged to love anyone.

That final accusation had been the hardest to take. It had made him face the fact that after five years of marriage, his wife still hadn't understood who he was. And he'd never considered himself damaged, not once the Andersons had taken him in.

He returned his attention to the screen, chose a tour that he decided Stefan would enjoy, then logged off the network and switched off the TV. He twisted the chair around so that he could watch Stefan sleep.

Strange, how life worked, he mused. He'd lost a wife, but in the process he'd gained a son. And Ellie had been wrong about his ability to love. David already loved this child.

But he didn't think he'd ever want to take another chance with a woman.

So he couldn't understand why images of Marina flickered through his mind. Marina baring her teeth at him. Marina with a smear of chocolate on the tip of her nose because she'd laughed as she'd been eating and hadn't been able to keep her hand steady. Marina bending to hug Stefan, oblivious to the way her blouse gaped open to display a shadow of cleavage…

Had she been oblivious?.Or had she left the buttons at her neckline unfastened deliberately? Was she hoping to tempt him into making a pass at her so she could claim he was a lecher and an unfit parent?

Or was he seeing Marina through the taint of Ellie's betrayal?

David tipped his head and swore silently at the ceiling. This was already complicated enough. He shouldn't be thinking about Marina at all, except as his adversary. Sure, she was a physically appealing woman, and at times he had to admit that he enjoyed her forthrightness. And he no longer had any doubts about the genuineness of her affection for Stefan, but the stakes were too high for personal feelings to enter into this. It was their second night on board. Only eight days remained for him to find a way to change her mind.

The sheets rustled. Instantly, David returned his attention to Stefan. He was starting to twitch in his sleep again. David waited, hoping it was just normal restlessness. It had been another exciting day for the child, and thanks to

Marina, Stefan had consumed enough chocolate to give a full-grown man a buzz for days.

Stefan drew his knees to his chest, his breathing accelerating. A shudder went through his shoulders.

David rose from the chair and went over to the bed. This was more than indigestion. It looked as if the bad dreams were happening again. That made three nights in a row that he knew of. "It's all right, Stefan," he murmured. "You're safe here."

Stefan rubbed his head against the pillow as if he were trying to burrow into it.

"Hey, buddy," David said. "It's okay. I'm here."

Unlike before, the calming words didn't appear to have any effect. Stefan's face crumpled as if he were about to cry. When he parted his lips, though, no sound came out. He gasped, his breath choking in his throat.

David stroked his forehead. "Stefan, it's only a dream. You're all right."

He twisted away from David's touch and curled into a ball. His entire body was shaking.

This was worse than the other times. David knelt on the bed, deciding to wake Stefan before the nightmare deepened. "Come on, son," David said, taking a firm grasp of Stefan's shoulder. "It's Dad. There's nothing to be afraid of."

Stefan's breath rushed out as if he were trying to scream but was unable to make a noise. The silence was more heartbreaking than sound would have been.

"Stefochka," David tried, remembering the names Marina had called him. "Stefanichka."

His eyes flew open. He panted, looking wildly around the room.

"Attaboy, son," David said. "See? You're okay. You're not alone."

Stefan's chest heaved as he looked at David. Before he drew another breath, he launched himself into David's embrace.

David closed his arms around Stefan's back and pulled him onto his lap. "There. It was only a bad dream. Nothing to be afraid of now."

Stefan turned his face to David's throat. *"Eevyerg,"* he whispered.

David didn't understand the word. *"Eevyerg?"* he repeated.

Stefan nodded fast, his hair brushing David's chin. He continued to whisper, his words punctuated by sobs. David guessed he must be describing his nightmare, telling his new dad what had frightened him.

But he was speaking in Russian.

The pocket dictionary on the dresser that David had been relying on wouldn't be enough now. Nor would an alphabet lesson from a kid's picture book. He had tried to minimize the communication issue when Marina had brought it up, but he'd known the lack of a common language between Stefan and him could be a serious problem.

And it didn't get more serious than this. Although David rocked him and tried to comfort him, Stefan wasn't calming down. He wasn't even sucking his thumb—his sobs were too violent. He trembled as he confided his fears, speaking with the breathless desperation of someone who had been bottling up the words for months.

It was Stefan's first act of real trust, a breakthrough in his relationship with David, and he needed more than a hug and a soothing tone of voice in response. His words were coming in a torrent, a big step for a boy who was normally so quiet, but how could David help him if he couldn't understand him?

The answer was obvious. Clasping Stefan securely in his arms, David rose to his feet, went to the phone and dialed the number of Marina's stateroom.

If asking for Marina's help as a translator gave her ammunition she could use against him in court later, then so be it. Their custody dispute was between the two of them, not Stefan, and there was no way in hell David was going to let this child suffer because of it.

CHAPTER FOUR

MARINA TUCKED THE phone between her shoulder and her ear so she could use both hands to dig through the heap of tour pamphlets and day-trip brochures that she'd left on the dining table. Her cell phone wouldn't work at sea, but the phones in her stateroom were cordless so they were almost as handy. She continued to dig until the trailing cuff of her pajama top caught the edge of a pamphlet and uncovered a corner of her sketchbook. "One moment, Rudolph. I remember seeing something here earlier."

"I believe Siiri faxed the contracts this morning, Marina."

She pushed her cuffs above her elbows and grabbed her sketchbook. As soon as she lifted it up, she spotted the documents her secretary had sent her. "Found them."

"Thank you. I'd like to draw your attention to the one for the beachwear. Second paragraph on the third page."

"Hang on." She tugged the pages from underneath her sketchbook, regarded the cluttered table for a moment, then carried the phone and the papers to the living room and sat cross-legged on the floor.

This penthouse suite was luxurious, one of only four this large on the ship, and it was roomier than many apartments Marina had lived in. In addition to the dining room table and chairs, there were armchairs, a sofa and a love seat in the living room, plus a king-size bed in the separate bedroom. While the olive-toned walls, white draperies and the pale wood tables and trim followed a more subdued color scheme than she would have chosen for herself, the overall effect was pleasing. Best of all, the size gave her plenty of space to spread out. She lined up the pages of the first contract on the carpet in front of her and leaned over to scan the third page.

Although she'd gone through the wording before she'd left Moscow, there were several potential trouble spots that Rudolph had noticed and had wanted to change.

She disliked this part of her work—she'd far prefer to spend her time with her sketchbook and her imagination— but the business side was a necessary evil if she wanted to keep her enterprise profitable. She'd relied on a handshake when she'd sold her first designs to a friend who ran a Moscow boutique and had wound up with only a fractional percentage of the price of the finished garments. It was scandalous how most corporations undervalued the artist. Without the creativity of the artist, there would be no product to sell.

Thankfully, it didn't take long to deal with the contracts. As soon as the business was finished, Rudolph turned to the reason she wasn't in her Moscow office in the first place. "Since I haven't been notified of a pending restraining order against you, I have to assume that Mr. Anderson is still willing to speak with you."

"Yes, he is." Marina inched backward along the carpet until she could lean her shoulders against the leather-covered love seat. "You needn't have worried."

"I always worry, Marina. That's why you pay me."

It was true. Along with his ability to be detached and

methodical, Rudolph's pessimism provided a good balance to her own nature. "Really, it's not going too badly. David's cooperating. He agreed that it would be best for Stefan if we could avoid court."

"Then do you want me to withdraw our petition?"

"Not yet. He hasn't agreed that I should have Stefan, only that we should discuss it."

"Are you making any progress?"

"I hope so."

"This is very unorthodox. I would far prefer it if you forgot about this and went through the proper channels."

She reached behind her to grab one of the throw pillows from the love seat and propped it behind her head. "You would get along well with David, Rudolph. He likes rules and schedules and has no flair for the dramatic at all. But he is trying to be nice to Stefan."

"Yes, I assumed he must be, or I would have been notified that you had thrown him overboard."

She gave a startled laugh. "There's still more than a week left. It might happen yet."

There was a pause. "It's good to hear you laugh, Marina. It's been a long time."

It had been nine months, she realized as she finished the call. From the time she'd learned of Olena's and Borya's deaths, she'd had little to smile about and no reason to laugh. She hadn't allowed herself time to grieve, either. Her life had revolved around her search for her nephew. Finding him at last had been like stepping suddenly from the dead of winter into a full-blown spring.

God, she wouldn't be able to bear it if she lost him again.

Leaving the contracts on the floor, she rolled to her feet and returned to the dining table. She sorted through the brochures until she found one with a map. Tomorrow the ship would stop in Dubrovnik, and according to David's schedule, he was planning to go on another tour. This would be the perfect time to demonstrate the benefits of all the business trips she'd taken. She hadn't been familiar with today's port of call, but she had visited Dubrovnik several times and could show Stefan places she knew he'd enjoy.

If Stefan lived with her, he could come along on her business trips. He would be exposed to countless cultures and languages; he could stand in the very spots where history had happened. What an education that would be— better than anything he could learn from David's books.

A sharp rapping sounded on the door of her stateroom.

Startled, Marina turned away from the table. She hadn't ordered anything from room service recently. There was an impressive variety of amenities that came free with the penthouse staterooms, but it was after midnight, too late for one of the cruise staff to be bringing more goodies or offering their services. Someone probably had the wrong door.

The knock came again, more insistent this time. "Marina?"

It was David's voice. She dropped the brochure and sprinted across the room. She was reaching for the doorknob when the door shook as if David had pounded it with his fist. She didn't bother checking the peephole before she opened the lock and yanked open the door.

It was David, but she almost didn't recognize him. He wore the same shirt that he'd had on all day, but it was wrinkled and the collar was crushed as if he'd retrieved it from a laundry bag. His normally neat hair was sticking out in damp clumps. His cheeks were darkened with the day's growth of beard stubble. Tension pulsed in his clenched jaw and in his tightly set lips and worry clouded his gaze.

All this she absorbed at a glance before her attention snapped to the child in his arms.

Stefan's eyes were puffy, tears streaked his cheeks, and the skin around his eyes and on his forehead was mottled with blotches that were almost as red as the pajamas he wore.

"Marina, I need your help," David said.

She grasped his forearm and pulled him over the threshold. She gave no thought to the late hour, or to how she was dressed. Not for a moment did she consider that David wasn't her friend, either. Her only concern was Stefan. "What's wrong?"

"He had another bad dream. I couldn't calm him down this time." He rubbed Stefan's back as he carried him into the living room. "He's afraid of something but I can't understand what he's saying so I hoped you could translate for me. I tried to call you but your phone was busy."

Marina shut the door and followed them. "I was talking to Rudolph. Stefan, what's the matter?" she asked, switching to Russian.

In reply, Stefan hiccuped and buried his face against David's neck.

Marina used her toes to shove the contracts that lay on the carpet out of David's path and waved him toward the love seat.

David sat, shifting Stefan to his lap. "See? Here's Aunt Nina. Everything will be fine."

Marina sat sideways on the love seat in the space that remained and placed her hand on Stefan's back. She asked him again what the matter was, but he was hiccuping too hard to speak.

David looked at Marina. "He was talking a mile a

minute before we left our cabin. He kept saying something that sounded like *eevyerg.*"

"That means monster," Marina said. "Like in the fairy tales. An ogre."

"There was more, but I couldn't understand him."

"I can't remember Olena saying that Stefan had many nightmares. He was a very happy child. This is probably because of what's happened since last summer. Even an adult could get nightmares after what Stefan's been through."

"He was trying to tell me what he was afraid of, Marina." David placed his hand over hers. "Whatever his monsters are, I want to help him fight them."

Even through the haze of her concern for Stefan, Marina couldn't help being aware of the difference in David. How could she have thought this man was passionless? The flashes of emotion that she'd glimpsed during the past two days were nothing compared to the raw anxiety she saw in him now.

"This is important," he said. His voice was rough, resonating with urgency. "Stefan needs to realize that someone will listen or he'll stop opening up. Please, try again."

She reversed her hand so that she could squeeze his fingers, then slid closer on the love seat until her knee pressed into his thigh. "Let me have him," she murmured.

David made no objection to either her offer or the way she'd worded it. He leaned back so she could slip her arms around her nephew, then helped her ease him onto her lap. It appeared that for tonight, at least, David wasn't her enemy.

Yet once she was holding Stefan, Marina felt a moment of uncertainty. Whenever she had visited her sister and her family, she'd only shared fun times with her nephew. Olena had been the one to take over whenever he'd gotten cranky or sleepy, and she hadn't missed an opportunity to point out how little Marina knew about handling children.

But this wasn't the time for Marina to dwell on her lack of maternal skills. As she usually did when faced with a problem, she followed her instincts. Placing her lips next to Stefan's ear, she hummed one of the tunes that his father used to play. Although her off-key humming was a poor substitute for a balalaika or Olena's wonderful voice, Stefan's sobs gradually slowed. She spoke to him in Russian, talking about ordinary things, like the shape of the chocolates he'd eaten that morning and the colors of the sailboats they'd spotted in the Katakolon harbor. When she asked him again what he'd dreamed about, he shuddered and finally started to talk.

David had been right. Stefan's nightmare had been about a monster. The creature he described sounded like a cross between a man and an ogre from an illustration in a fairy-tale book. He was tall and thin, and had a long black raincoat that turned into wings. He hissed when he spoke and he spat blood. His face was pale and shiny, and he had a scar like a sickle carved into one cheek.

A chill went through Marina as she translated Stefan's words for David. It was little wonder her nephew was so upset. The monster he'd dreamed up would probably give *her* nightmares.

DAVID PACED PAST the leather living room furniture and around the dining table to the door of the veranda. Marina's suite would hold three staterooms the size of his and Stefan's, so it provided plenty of space for him to move. That was good, because he was too restless to sit.

Logically, he knew it probably had been only a dream as Marina maintained. Any child could get nightmares.

Yet what normal nightmare caused the panic that Stefan had displayed? His description of the monster had seemed too detailed for a dream. It had sounded as if he were remembering someone specific. If that was true, then the worst thing David could do would be to dismiss the scarred man in the raincoat as a figment of Stefan's imagination.

He knew what it was like not to be believed. He remembered the helplessness. It had left him powerless and completely alone. He'd promised to protect Stefan.

On the other hand, he had to admit that he could be reading too much into this nightmare. Stefan's fears had stirred up David's own childhood monsters, so David was far from objective when it came to this topic. Yes, he was a new father who was eager to be a good parent, but he didn't want to upset Stefan needlessly by overreacting. Without something more substantial to go on, it probably would be better for both of them if he let this incident slide.

Besides, what could he do? Demand the police investigate a child's dream?

"My nephew has a vivid imagination, David." Marina took two bottles of cola from the refrigerator, held one out to him and lifted an eyebrow in question. When he shook his head, she put one bottle back and poured the other into a tall glass. "He could be an artist someday."

That might be all there was to it. David glanced at the love seat where Stefan was tucked beneath a down duvet. The child had fallen asleep on Marina's lap an hour ago, and David hadn't wanted to risk disturbing him by taking him back to their stateroom right away. He'd found no reason to refuse when Marina had suggested they let him stay where he was for a while.

It probably hadn't been the smartest decision he could

have made, but he'd been thinking of Stefan, not the impact this night could have on his custody case.

Or on his libido.

David raked one hand through his hair and rubbed the back of his neck. That was the other reason for his restlessness. He'd done his best to ignore it, but he'd been physically aware of Marina from the moment she'd opened the door to him. It was a natural reaction. It was the middle of the night and his emotions were scrambled. Just because he'd become a father didn't mean he'd stopped being a man.

Fine, so Marina was an attractive woman. He'd accepted that already. He'd have to be blind not to notice how those loose satin pajamas she wore flowed over her curves like water, and how the rich, burgundy color brought out hidden hints of copper in her hair. She was barefoot, and toenails painted fuschia peeked out from beneath the wide cuffs of her pajama bottoms, yet she carried herself with as much confidence as when she wore a dress and heels.

To David, though, her most appealing feature wasn't anything physical. It was the love that had shone from her face as she had hummed to his son.

Finding *that* attractive didn't make sense. She did love his son, and because of that she was determined to take him away. David wasn't fool enough to believe that this unspoken truce they seemed to have stumbled into was going to last. Now that the crisis was over and Stefan was sleeping peacefully, Marina was bound to use the situation to her advantage. She was too clever not to.

Satin whispered on satin as she carried her glass past the dining table and joined him at the balcony door.

David caught a whiff of apples. He watched her lips purse as she took a sip of her drink and he remembered what she'd said about chocolate being like kisses. No one could stop with just one.

Would she be as passionate about a man as she was about a child?

Damn, he had no business wondering that.

"You're free to leave Stefan here for the rest of the night, David. I can bring him back to you in the morning."

He yanked his mind back to business. Her offer seemed generous, but he couldn't afford to take it at face value. She'd said she'd been talking to her lawyer when he'd tried to phone her earlier. They could have been discussing her custody suit strategy for all he knew. "No, thanks, Marina. I'll give him a few more minutes and then take him back."

"He's no trouble. He might want to talk again when he wakes up. It would be best for him if he was with someone who spoke Russian."

"I appreciate your offer, but I am his father and we'll find a way to manage."

She scowled at him over her glass. "You're sounding starchy again."

"Starchy?"

"Like a teacher with a schedule to keep. I was not trying to score a point, David. I'm thinking of Stefan."

"Of course."

"I remember having nightmares during times of change. Stefan's been through too many changes. He lost his home and his parents, and now he's being taken away from his culture and native tongue. He would feel more comfortable with me."

"For someone who's not trying to score points, you're hitting plenty of serves."

"What does that mean? Is that some kind of American baseball analogy?"

"More like volleyball or tennis. Don't you follow sports?"

"No."

"Most boys love sports."

She lifted her chin. "For Stefan, I will learn."

"At the high school where I work, I teach physical education along with mathematics. I can help Stefan learn to play any game he wants."

"Well, I can hire him a coach. I can buy him his own baseball team if he wanted one."

"You can't buy self-esteem for a child. He has to earn it."

"Have you ever raised a child?"

"No, but—"

"Then you have no more qualifications than I do."

"I know that a child doesn't need your wealth to be happy. Money can't buy the things that really matter."

She gulped a mouthful of her cola and swallowed hard. "So I've been told."

"By whom?"

"My sister. Score one for you, Mr. Anderson." She reached past him to shove open the sliding door and stepped onto the balcony. She set her glass on a low table and walked to the railing. Crossing her arms on the rail, she squared her shoulders and lifted her face into the breeze.

David could see he'd scored a point, but he hadn't meant to hit a nerve. He followed her outside, leaving the door open behind him so that he'd be able to hear Stefan. The penthouse staterooms were on a higher deck than the ones that held the lower-priced cabins. Except for the breeze, the only sounds were the distant *shush* of the water and the low vibration of the ship's engines. "Marina…"

She flicked her fingers at him without turning around. "Let me know when you're ready to leave."

He knew he should go. There was no practical purpose to prolonging his stay, yet he moved beside her anyway. The night spread in front of them, an endless expanse of starry black over moon-dappled silver, giving the illusion that they were floating in a world of their own. And he had another one of those crazy impulses to reach out and pull Marina into his arms.

David drew in a bracing lungful of salt-tanged air, then clasped his hands and leaned his forearms on the railing next to Marina. "Your money was a source of friction between you and your sister, wasn't it?" he asked.

"That is a good guess."

"It was two plus two. I did mention I also teach math, didn't I?"

She sighed. "Well, you're right. My wealth was one of the things Olena and I didn't agree about. I tried to share it, but she didn't want any of my money. She and Borya were happy just as they were."

David wasn't surprised that she'd answered him. She was too forthright not to. "What was Borya like?" he asked.

"It's difficult to describe him in a few words. He used to remind me of a rock on the seashore that glistens in the sun, solid and lively at the same time."

"I want you to know that I'm not trying to take his place with Stefan," David said. "That's why I asked him to call me dad instead of the Russian word for father."

"Good." She glanced at him. "Borya would have appreciated that."

"What did he do for a living?"

"He was a fisherman like my father."

"Stefan likes boats. That must be why."

"Yes, Stefan loved Borya's boat. He enjoyed seeing the other ships in the harbor, too. There weren't as many as in my father's day, though. The big fish canneries in Murmansk shut down after the Soviet Union dissolved and the central funding for remote areas was cut off."

"How did Stefan's parents manage?"

"Borya had to sell his catch to foreign factory ships. He'd be gone for months at a time, and Olena had to scrape by with next to nothing, but still they refused to accept any help from me. Borya wouldn't take charity any more than he'd turn to smuggling to supplement his income."

"Smuggling?"

"In any port there are ways to earn extra money if you own a boat, but not for Borya. He was a proud man, and an honest one. Olena loved him from the moment they met. Their child was born from that love." Her voice turned husky. "She was the rich sister, not I."

"I'm sorry, Marina. I keep forgetting that Stefan wasn't the only one who lost his family in that car accident. You did, too. It must have been a blow."

She swept her arm toward the sea. "It was as if I'd been cut adrift. I felt lost, as if I were wandering across the surface of life without a home port."

The description was dramatic, but David realized that was how Marina expressed herself. There were no half measures with her.

"I felt the same after my parents died," she went on. "I know I didn't get home often but my family was my anchor. I wouldn't have had the courage to do any of the things I've done if I hadn't felt my family with me, in here," she said, bringing her hand to her heart.

He knew what she meant. He owed everything he was to the Andersons.

"Stefan is the only family I have left. That is another reason why he's so precious to me. Without him, I am…alone." She inhaled shakily. "I have been babbling."

"I'd call it being open with your feelings."

She turned her head to look at him. Moonlight reflected from the water, giving her eyes a silver sheen. The effect suited her, David thought. Her moods were like quicksilver. "Tell me about your family, David. Do you have any sisters?"

He hesitated. He had considered the size of the Anderson family to be one of the biggest factors in favor of his custody of Stefan. He'd thought any child would be better off having the security of dozens of relatives rather than one lone aunt. He didn't feel right about pointing that out to Marina now.

"What?" she asked. "You can question me about my sister but I can't ask you about yours?"

"No, not at all. I have one older sister and two younger ones. My brothers are both older than me."

"You have three sisters and two brothers?"

"Yes. Blanche, Betty-Lou, Keisha, Levar and Juan."

She appeared to digest that for a while. "Your parents chose very different names to give their children."

"The only name my parents gave us was Anderson."

"I don't understand."

"We were all adopted."

The breeze blew a lock of hair across her cheek. She brushed it aside, then pressed her fingertips to her mouth and shook her head slowly back and forth.

"What's wrong?" he asked.

"You were adopted," she mumbled. "I hadn't thought of that. Is that why you wanted to adopt a child yourself?"

"There were many reasons why I went that route. One was that my own experience made me realize it would work. I had been in several foster homes before the Andersons took me. They formally adopted me three years later."

"But they're not your real parents."

"Not by blood, but in every other way, they are." He twisted to look through the door to the love seat where Stefan slept.

And as he watched his son, the memory of his own first few nights in the Anderson house rose to his mind. He hadn't slept well, either, but that hadn't been only from the nightmares. It had been because his wounds had started stinging whenever he'd rolled onto his back.

She followed his gaze. "That's why you're so protective of Stefan. You were an orphan like him."

"I wasn't an orphan, Marina."

"What do you mean?"

He debated how much to tell her and decided there was no reason to sugarcoat things. If her lawyer was any good, he had probably already started an investigation into David's past. The official records were sealed, but there were plenty of people who knew the truth, so it wouldn't be hard to dig up. Coming clean was probably the best way to deflect any points her lawyer might try to make from his background.

"I never met my father," he said. "I heard he worked the rodeo circuit and met my mother when he was passing through Tulsa. She was fifteen when she got pregnant and her family kicked her out."

"My God. How did she manage?"

"She traveled east with some idea of making it big on Broadway, but she ended up in Burlington. I don't remember much about my early years, except having to sit quietly behind the lunch counter while she worked. She was a waitress. When I was five she pinned a note to my shirt, left me in the diner at the end of her shift and never came back."

"She *left* you?"

"I can't blame her. She wasn't much more than a kid herself. She wasn't ready to be a mother."

"And her family, your grandparents? They wouldn't help?"

"No. They were ashamed of both her and me."

She gripped his arm with both hands. "You were an innocent child! It is unthinkable!"

"I survived."

"Children are treasures. That is so wrong! Children belong with their family."

"People don't need to be related by blood to form a family. I'm living proof of that."

"But you had relatives, didn't you? They should have helped."

David looked at where she touched him. He wasn't surprised by her outrage. She had strong feelings about family and would be quick to rise to any child's defense. He shouldn't take the physical contact personally, no matter how good it felt. "Being a relative doesn't automatically make someone a fit parent."

She paused. "Are you still talking about yourself, or are you talking about Stefan?"

"It applies to both of us. A blood relative isn't always the right parent."

Muttering what sounded like a Russian oath, she released his arm and smacked him in the chest. "You always have to be my enemy. Can't you forget our argument for one minute?"

He caught her wrist. "You know I can't."

"Why?"

"Because that's the only reason you're here."

"Here? What do you mean?"

"On the ship. In my life. Talking to me like this. It's why we met. We *are* enemies, Marina. Neither of us should forget that."

Her eyes gleamed. This time she was the one who looked at the place where he touched her. Her pajama cuff had fallen to her elbow, exposing her slender forearm in a way that was more enticing than if she'd been sleeveless. Against the feminine fairness of her skin, his broad, tanned hand should have looked out of place. It didn't. It looked…right.

He stroked his thumb across the underside of her wrist. He could feel her pulse accelerate, beating with the same excitement as his own. "You should step back, Marina."

She met his gaze squarely. "You should let go, David."

It was as much a challenge as their arguments were. And it seemed just as natural. Without thinking, he curled her hand toward his chest and drew her closer until her bare toes nudged his shoes. A breeze gusted around them, whispering her satin pajamas against the stiff cotton twill of his pants. The wayward lock of hair that she'd been brushing away from her cheek wafted across the side of his neck. The aroma of apples teased his tongue, along with a sweet, earthy scent that wasn't from any perfume.

She parted her lips. But whether it was to make a protest, or an invitation, he never found out. A flash of movement in the living room caught his eye. Stefan was awake and sitting up, and he was staring straight at them.

David realized he should have been grateful for the interruption.

Yet long after he'd taken his son back to their stateroom, he still hadn't convinced himself that he was.

CHAPTER FIVE

THE MODEST CAFÉ was miles from the medieval stone walls of the Old City that drew tourists to Dubrovnik. There were no picturesque fountains or churches on this street, no trendy boutiques, no scenic vistas. The sunrise that spread over the red rooftops dotting the city's hills hadn't yet penetrated the shadows here. Yellowed ceiling bulbs glowed over a mixture of chrome chairs with vinyl seats and wooden tables the color of mud. It was dim, crowded with dockworkers and rife with the odor of fish.

As usual, Ilya Fedorovich gave no thought to his surroundings, other than scanning the room for anything that looked out of place. It was a reflex action. The odds that any law enforcement agency would be looking for him here in Croatia were slim. Only the Russian deckhand he was meeting knew where Ilya was, and he understood what would happen if he talked.

Ilya took a table in a corner and placed his back to the wall. He ordered coffee so the waitress would leave him to his business, but he didn't touch the cup. He had no need for caffeine. Already he could feel his blood warm deliciously with the prospect of a kill. *Alexandra's Dream* had docked an hour ago, following the itinerary for the cruise to the minute.

He ran his tongue along the inside of his cheek, trying to contain his impatience as he watched the door. Five minutes later a short, dark-haired man in a navy windbreaker entered and walked over to his table.

"The boy you're looking for is on board," the man said, sliding into the chair across from him.

Ilya studied the deckhand to make sure he wasn't saying only what he knew Ilya wanted to hear. He'd first met Misha in Moscow a decade ago when the man had been working in an auto repair shop. Misha hadn't asked questions as he'd fixed some bullet holes in Ilya's car, but that had likely been due to cowardice more than intelligence. He'd started working the cruise ships as a way to avoid a demanding girlfriend.

He was a weakling. A bullet would have solved the girlfriend problem easily. But since Misha's current position was on *Alexandra's Dream,* he was a valuable weakling. "Do you have any proof he is there?" Ilya demanded.

"*Da.* I got a friend of mine from the cruise staff to print out the passenger list." He withdrew a folded sheaf of papers from inside his windbreaker and laid them on the table. "See, he's right here on deck seven," he said, jabbing a blunt fingertip at a line that had been circled. "David Anderson and Stefan Gorsky. Anderson's the guy who's his new father. They probably didn't have time to change the kid's name to Anderson yet so his real one would be on the travel documents."

Ilya picked up the papers and slipped them inside his overcoat, his hand steady in spite of the sudden jump in his pulse. At last. This confirmed the information Sergei had given him, and he now knew exactly where his target was. It was only a matter of time before his job would be complete. His record would remain perfect. The ache would ease. "Misha, who else did you tell about this?"

"What? I didn't tell anyone."

"Then who printed the passenger list?"

"She's no one."

"**Another** girlfriend?"

"Okay, yeah, but I didn't tell her why I needed it. I don't want any trouble."

Beads of sweat had formed on Misha's forehead. It wasn't that warm in the café. "Then why are you so nervous?"

"I, uh, couldn't get you a card."

Ilya frowned. Confirming that the Gorsky child was on the ship was only the preliminary step. The next was finding a way on board himself. That was the surest method to reach his target: once he was on the ship, he could eliminate the boy as he slept. He'd need to kill the new father, too, yet by the time anyone found the bodies the ship would be at the next port of call and Ilya would be long gone.

But getting on a cruise ship wasn't as simple as boarding a train or a ferry. It was too late to buy a ticket. Visitors weren't allowed. The best method to gain access to the ship would be as a crew member, which was why he'd ordered Misha to get him one of the crew identity cards. "You'll have to bring me on board some other way."

"I can't. The security is too tight."

"There are always holes."

"No, I'm telling you, there aren't any. The chief of security knows what he's doing. Gideon Dayan's more than just a cop. I heard rumors he's ex-Masad. And Captain Pappas is a real hard-ass. This is the ship's maiden voyage, and he's running everything by the book, like he's got something to prove. No one can get on board without going through all the identity checks."

"That's not what I wanted to hear, Misha."

Misha rubbed his index finger over his upper lip. Sweat had appeared there, too. "Look, it's not my fault. I did what I could."

Ilya regarded the deckhand in disgust. The man was too weak to follow a simple order. And his ID would be useless—he was too short and swarthy for Ilya to try to pass himself off in his place. With the end so near, this setback was difficult to tolerate. The alternative to eliminating the target on the ship would be to follow the ship from port to port and take out the boy when he came ashore. It could be done, but it would be riskier.

"He's only a kid," Misha said.

"What's your point?"

"Why do you want to kill him? If he was a witness or something, he's too young for anyone to believe him."

Ilya moved his hand from the pocket where he'd put the passenger list to the one where he kept his gun. Misha's cowardice made him easy to coerce, but cowards could prove dangerous when they lost their nerve. They could forget where their loyalty lay and talk to the wrong people. They became a liability that had to be eliminated, and Misha had just outlived his usefulness. "My job is my business."

"I know. I'm sorry. It's just that…"

"What, Misha?" With a deftness made possible from years of practice, Ilya relied only on his sense of touch as he fitted the silencer to the end of the barrel and screwed it into place. "You seem nervous."

"Sorry, I don't mean any offense."

"Speak your mind. We're in a public place. Would I have asked you here if I'd wanted to do you harm?"

Misha glanced around, then returned his gaze to Ilya's as if he'd somehow found reassurance in the roomful of disinterested strangers. "From what I heard, the boy's going to America. That's a long way from your turf. Maybe it would be easier to let him be."

Ilya's lips curved as he stroked his finger along the trigger guard.

Misha must have mistaken his expression for a smile. He leaned closer and crossed his arms on the table, his words coming more rapidly. "The kid will be on the other side of the world. He'll be no threat. It wouldn't hurt you to show some mercy. He couldn't be five years old yet."

Ilya tongued the ridge of scar tissue that was a souvenir of the only time he'd made the error of showing mercy. Misha was wrong. Mercy did hurt. It was as lethal to a man's survival as a conscience.

He reached across the table to clasp the deckhand's shoulder in what would appear to a casual observer as a friendly gesture. Holding him in place, he brought his gun from his pocket beneath the table and squeezed the trigger twice.

The silenced shots were lost in the clink of crockery and silverware and the hum of conversation from the other patrons. Misha appeared puzzled at first when he couldn't draw any breath. He looked down, but there was little to see. The holes in his jacket, and the blood that dripped on the table, were difficult to spot in the dimness of the café. Ilya had angled his shots with precision through the diaphragm so the bullets would have torn the maximum amount of lung tissue. Most of the blood would be leaking into Misha's chest cavity, not out of it, pumping into his lungs and cutting off his oxygen with each beat of his heart. He didn't have the strength for more than a low gurgle before he passed out.

Ilya returned his gun to his coat pocket, guided Misha forward and arranged his forearms on the table to pillow his head as if he were sleeping. This kill wasn't planned. It was a matter of necessity more than honor.

Yet anticipation rushed through his veins anyway. His mouth watered. The familiar red haze was already building on the edge of his vision. It would be a while before anyone realized that something was amiss. He had time....

Ilya thrust his hand back into the pocket with his gun and stroked his thumb along the warmth of the freshly fired barrel. Then he bit the edge of his scar to fill his mouth with the taste of blood and waited for Misha to die.

THE TAXI WOVE through the traffic toward Dubrovnik's harbor, gaining only a few feet before it screeched to a halt behind a bus. David checked his watch and drummed his fingers on the armrest of the door.

Marina gritted her teeth. She had found that was the only way to maintain her smile now that her cheeks were aching. It had been a long day of being polite. "It's not far," she said. "I think I saw the ship's smokestack before that bus got in the way."

"The ship leaves at six."

"Yes, I am aware of the schedule."

"There are reasons people abide by schedules, Marina. It's to prevent situations like these."

She crossed her arms tightly so that she wouldn't be

tempted to hit him. But even if she did, he would probably smile at her and pretend she was swatting a fly for him.

He was doing his best to be Mr. Bland today. He'd been like that from the time he and Stefan had met her in the lobby so they could disembark for their tour of Dubrovnik. There had been no trace of the rumpled, unshaven, passionate man who had been in her stateroom yesterday. In fact, he was as stiff and stodgy as he'd been at the start of the cruise. If it hadn't been for the dark circles under his eyes, she might have thought the night before hadn't happened.

Was she the only one who couldn't forget what it had felt like to stand together in the moonlight? Had she imagined the current that had sparked between them? She had been close, oh, so close, to yanking his face down to hers and…

And what? *Kissing* him?

"The tour I booked would have returned us to the pier by four," he said.

How could she contemplate kissing him when most of the time she wanted to smack him? He was sounding more and more like a teacher chastising a student. "The tour you booked would have bored us to death."

"A responsible parent plans ahead. Stability is important to a child."

"He had fun."

"He's exhausted."

This was true. Marina had started with a vague idea of showing Stefan the breathtaking architecture and the many fountains of the old city, but after he'd seen the cannons and played on the wall, she had expanded her plan. For the remainder of the day they had hopped buses and taxis to zigzag across the city, stopping to explore whatever had caught Stefan's interest, whether it had been the carved stone ballusters of an ancient abbey or the gaudy painted handcart of a chestnut vendor. They'd been guided by whim, not a map.

She unfolded her arms so that she could stroke Stefan's forehead. He was sound asleep on the seat between her and David, his jaw slack and his mouth open with the boneless relaxation only the young could manage. His head had fallen back against David's arm, so when she touched Stefan's hair, her fingertips grazed David's biceps.

She didn't bother telling herself to ignore the contact. She'd been noticing that muscle all day. The cuff of David's shapeless, boring yellow golf shirt hadn't been able to conceal the well-defined curves of his upper arms. He had the solid, lean build of an athlete.

He'd said he taught physical education and that his father—his real father—had been in a rodeo. That explained both his toned physique and his resemblance to a cowboy. And as she'd discovered yesterday, he could indeed be gentle when he caressed a woman. She'd felt that brush of his thumb from her wrist to her bare toes.

Yet it had been his story that had touched her far more deeply than his caress. He was an adopted son, and he wanted to adopt a son of his own. Instead of turning him bitter, his early years had made him want to reach out to another child as the Andersons had reached out to him. She would find that admirable…

If only it wasn't *this* child.

She stroked Stefan's hair again, letting her forefinger trace the tempting, square-angled dip between David's biceps and his elbow before she withdrew her hand and turned her face to the window.

We are enemies, Marina. Neither of us should forget that.

The words he'd said to her the night before had been hanging between them all day. Of course, she knew he'd been right to remind her. She'd already told him the same thing. She'd spent most of the night reminding herself of it. She had dark circles of her own to match David's, only she'd been able to hide hers behind makeup and sunglasses.

"There are some sharp edges on the music box you bought Stefan," David said. "I'd like to bend them down before you give it to him."

She could no longer clench her teeth—her jaw was beginning to ache like her cheeks—so she started nibbling at her upper lip. She opened the bag that sat on the floor beside her feet and took out the gift he referred to.

It was a beautiful piece, but it wasn't meant to be a child's toy. The box was fashioned of cobalt-blue glass and covered by a silver filigree. The fine metal wires did stick up at the corners, and she realized now that it might prick Stefan's fingers or get caught on his clothes. She hadn't thought of that when she'd bought it. She'd spotted it in the window of a jewelry shop as they were walking past, and it had been too appealing to resist.

She tilted the music box toward the late-day sunshine that slanted through the car window beside her. Two tiny silver lovebirds were perched on a wire branch that rose from the center of the box. Stefan had laughed out loud when she had wound up the box and the birds had moved their heads to the music.

The tune was a sad one, though. It was "Lara's Theme" from the movie version of Pasternak's tragic novel, *Doctor Zhivago,* a tale about two lovers destined to be separated. In Russian literature, most love stories ended badly.

She put the box back in the bag without playing it and handed the bag to David. "He loves music."

"Yes. It was a nice gift. It's just—"

"Not safe. Not appropriate. Not sensible. Too extravagant. I know. I've heard it before."

"Marina…"

"Are you *trying* to make yourself unlikable?"

"I don't know what you mean."

"You must." She draped her arm across the back of the seat as she twisted to face him. "I saw the real David last night. He wasn't obsessed with schedules or how things ought to be. He was a kind man. He listened to me talk about my family and he talked about his own. He let me see how deeply he cared for my nephew."

"My son," he corrected.

"See? All day you haven't missed an opportunity to make me dislike you."

"I'm the same person."

"Sure, in there," she said, poking her finger in the center of his chest. "But here?" She pinched a fold of his golf shirt between her thumb and forefinger as if it was something distasteful. "You're Mr. Perfect Parent who doesn't miss one single opportunity for scoring points."

He looked at her hand and curled his fingers around the armrest on the door. "And you don't?"

"Me?" She pressed her hand to the skin beneath her throat.

His gaze followed her gesture. A muscle twitched in his cheek. "Don't act innocent. You hijacked the tour I planned so you could show off. You spent every minute since we left the ship pointing out how much you know."

"I am familiar with Dubrovnik, as well as many other European cities."

"Yes. And you understand Croatian and God knows how many other languages."

"Only four, not counting Russian."

"And you made history sound interesting to a five-year-old."

"That's because it wasn't scheduled in a lesson."

"And you made Stefan laugh. In four days, I haven't heard him laugh like that, but your silly, whimsical, completely inappropriate gift made him laugh."

"Yes, it did. Do you have a problem with that, too?"

"No."

"Because sometimes children need more than…" She stopped. "No?" she repeated.

David smiled. It wasn't like the polite, cheek-cramping smiles they had been exchanging all day. This one was real. It brought out the cowboy grooves that framed his mouth and deepened the tiny crinkles beside his eyes. It was a smile from the man inside that boring, baggy golf shirt.

"Thank you, Marina," he murmured. "Stefan's laughter was the best gift you could have given us."

She was grateful for her sunglasses. David wouldn't be able to see the moisture that came to her eyes.

Damn, she wished she *could* dislike him. That would make fighting him so much easier. Moments like these completely disarmed her.

How was she supposed to prove she was a better parent for Stefan when David was so obviously a good one, too? Yet every time she found something she admired or respected about him, she felt as if she were being disloyal to Stefan.

The bus in front of them lurched forward suddenly. Marina braced her hand on the back of the taxi driver's seat and waved her other arm at the space that had opened to his left, urging him to take advantage of it. She promised to double his fare if he got them to the pier before the ship sailed. He gunned the engine and jolted past the bus.

The motion woke Stefan. He looked around blankly, his eyelids heavy, until he focused on Marina.

"Almost there, Stevovovichki," she said.

He popped his thumb into his mouth.

David met her gaze over Stefan's head. "He's probably hungry."

"Yes, I know. An early dinner at five-thirty at the Garden Terrace on the Artemis deck, item number eight on today's schedule." Marina reached into her purse and pulled out a piece of chocolate wrapped in gold foil. "This should help tide him over until we get there."

"Ever hear of nutrition, or don't they have that word in Russian?"

She flicked her fingers at him and unwrapped the foil.

Stefan withdrew his thumb and filled his mouth with the chocolate. His cheeks bulging as he chewed, he got on his knees and twisted to look out the back window.

"We'll be lucky if he doesn't throw up," David muttered. "Sitting backward in a moving car, having sweets on an empty stomach."

"He's a good traveler," Marina said. She wasn't going to tell David about the other times she'd stuffed Stefan full of candy and run around with him until he'd thrown up. "He's from a long line of fishermen. It would take more than this to give him motion sickness."

The taxi turned a corner and accelerated downhill. Marina took Stefan by the shoulders and made him sit on the seat. Now that they were picking up speed, she wished there were seat belts in this cab. She also wished that she had paid closer attention to the time so that they wouldn't have needed to hurry. David was right about the value of schedules, especially when it concerned children.

Not that she was going to admit that to him, either. He was making a good enough case for himself as it was. He certainly didn't need her help.

They reached the pier with no time to spare. Marina added a generous tip to the doubled fare as David picked up the bag with the music box and helped Stefan slide out of the car. The taxi had dropped them off close to the dock, but they still had to pass through the harbor security before they could get on the ship. As they had all day, David took one of Stefan's hands while Marina took the other. They'd gone no more than three steps when Stefan started to tremble.

Marina's first thought was that he had a stomach cramp from the chocolate. But then she realized he wasn't doubled over or holding his side, he was looking behind them.

"Hey, what's wrong?" David asked. He squatted beside Stefan and held out his arms. "Want me to carry you?"

Stefan looked from Marina to David. "See monster."

"What? No, son, that was only—"

"Monster," he repeated. *"Eevyerg!"* He tugged their hands, trying to pull them away from the pavement where the taxi had dropped them.

"That was only a dream," Marina told him in Russian. "It wasn't real. There's no monster here, Stefan. Nothing to be afraid of."

He stamped his feet and tugged their hands harder.

David scooped Stefan into his arms. "Don't you worry about monsters, Stefan," he said, heading into the cruise terminal. "They won't come near you as long as I'm around. I promise."

Marina looked behind them, but of course there was no monster there. Only more taxis dropping off other passengers and a pair of uniformed policemen walking toward a parked police car. Beyond them, a delivery truck was maneuvering around a group of husky men who were likely dockworkers. For an instant she caught a glimpse of a tall man with a pale face and a long black overcoat on the far side of the truck....

That must have been what had upset Stefan, she decided, turning to catch up with David. The child was hungry and tired, he'd seen the man with the pale face and the black coat and his imagination had done the rest.

FROM HIS VANTAGE POINT at the bow railing, Mike O'Connor wouldn't have been able to see the tall man in the black coat who watched the ship, but he did see the police car. It gave him the creeps. Even though he knew he was well disguised in these priest's clothes, he found himself holding his breath until he saw the car pull away.

All right. They hadn't been here for him.

"Did you pick the thing up?"

Mike turned to look at Giorgio. The "thing" was a twenty-seven-hundred-year-old Athenian gold pin from the Geometric Period, but Mike had already learned that his partner had little appreciation of the objects they were smuggling. "Yes, I picked it up."

"Where is it?"

"I put it with the rest of my collection."

"In your stateroom?"

"That's the best camouflage. No one's going to suspect there's a genuine article among the fakes."

Giorgio smiled and sucked in his stomach as a pair of

young women walked past. As soon as they were out of earshot, he turned back to Mike. "You can't keep that up for long. You should let me stash the merchandise in a lifeboat the way I wanted to."

"Lifeboats are inspected. Anything you put there would be discovered within days."

"Someone's bound to notice your collection is growing."

"Let them. Who's going to get suspicious if the charming Father Connelly feeds his antiquities habit?" He followed the progress of the women until they were greeted by a pair of men. "After all, what other pleasures in life are there for a man sworn to celibacy?"

"Speaking of pleasures, have you seen the librarian? Ariana Bennett's a fox."

"Careful, Giorgio. I think there's more going on there than she lets on."

"Why?"

"She's smart. She's also been leaving the ship as often as I have."

"So? It's her first sailing. She's playing tourist. Just because you're stuck in that collar doesn't mean I can't look for some fun, *Father* Connelly."

Mike sighed. "I noticed a pair of local cops came on board earlier. What was that all about?"

"One of the deckhands got himself shot this morning. The cops were here to talk to the captain about it."

"Murdered? That's going to tighten up security."

"Don't worry. He wasn't killed here. It happened in some dive near the harbor."

"Well, that's not as bad."

"From what I heard, it was probably some personal score."

"Does that mean they know who did it?"

"Not so far. It was in one of those places where no one wants to notice anything. I'm guessing it was personal because the deckhand was Russian. You know how they are."

"I don't care why he was killed or who did it, as long as it doesn't bring any more law enforcement agents to this ship." His gaze strayed back to the direction the police car had taken. "We've got a sweet deal going here. A complication like a murder investigation is the last thing we need."

CHAPTER SIX

THE HELIOS DECK was the topmost one on the ship, and it provided a wide variety of diversions, from a fitness center to a spa. Under other circumstances, David would have been making full use of the exercise equipment. He wasn't accustomed to going this many days without a good workout. That was probably one of the reasons why he was feeling so tense.

But the main reason his muscles were tightening and his fingers were closing into fists wasn't a lack of exercise. It was the woman who was racing toward him.

It had been impossible to miss Marina's arrival. She'd burst onto the deck at a run, her sandaled feet skidding across the wood and her skirt flaring around her calves. She was wearing pink today, the hue as fresh as a sunrise, yet as always, it wasn't her clothes that made her so noticeable, it was her energy. Two men on the putting green bumped into each other as they turned to watch her go by. One of the players on the tennis courts smiled to her as she passed, oblivious to the serve that went whizzing by his racket.

David knew how they felt. Marina could distract anyone. She looked magnificent in the morning sunlight, like an embodiment of the breeze that swept in from the water. Her hair streamed behind her, vibrant and untamed, as unrepentantly feminine as the clothes she wore. It defied containment, just as she defied schedules. It tempted him to touch, to caress, to wind a lock around his hands and rub it across his lips….

Damn. He should have booked time on a treadmill instead of waiting for her. He leaned back on the bench, stretched out his legs and crossed them at the ankles. He hoped the relaxed pose would fool his body into loosening up.

"Where's Stefan?" she demanded as soon as she reached him. "Is he all right? I know I'm late but you were supposed to be at the children's center. What are you doing out here?"

"Stefan's fine. He's in there." David cocked his thumb toward the glass wall beside him.

She stepped over his legs and peered through the window. "Where? I don't see him."

"He's with the group in the circle beside the piano. And that *is* the children's center. These benches are for any parents who might want to check on their kids." He looked past Marina. The ship offered daily programs for every age group, so he'd had no trouble finding something suitable for Stefan. Although little sound came through the thick glass, David could see his son was beginning to participate. Language wasn't a barrier to kids. They were doing what appeared to be a clapping game, and Stefan was rocking from side to side with the rest of the children as they followed the rhythm of a song.

"Shouldn't you be in there with him?" Marina asked.

David had wrestled with the same thought himself, but had decided a brief separation would be healthy for Stefan. It would show him he could trust David to come back. "He'll be able to see me if he gets anxious, but I don't think that will happen. As soon as he saw the piano he let go of my hand and made straight for it."

"One of Olena's neighbors had a piano. Stefan used to love to hear her play."

"Kids need their space. It builds confidence. They also need to be with other kids their own age."

"But—"

"I explained Stefan's situation to the girl who's leading the group. She knows I'm right out here and will call me if necessary."

"Who? That teenager with the streaked hair? She looks too young to know anything about children."

"I assure you, Gemma Slater is well qualified and she struck me as quite responsible. She's the granddaughter of the man who owns this cruise line, and she's pursuing a career in early childhood development."

Marina made a noise that sounded like *humph* and regarded David over her shoulder. "You said these benches are for the parents, so where's everyone else?"

He nodded his head toward the putting green and tennis courts. "The other parents are likely taking advantage of their free time."

"Now that I'm here, I can watch Stefan. You don't have to stay."

Yes, but I would rather spend my free time with you than with an exercise machine.

The thought took him off guard. He couldn't deny it, though. In spite of the ongoing friction between them, he had to admit that Marina was stimulating company. He also was certain that if he *hadn't* been here, she would have taken advantage of the situation by attempting to hijack Stefan's morning the way she'd hijacked yesterday's tour.

That's why he'd given Gemma Slater strict orders not to release Stefan to anyone except him. "I'm enjoying the fresh air," he replied.

She looked around as if only now realizing what an excellent view their location provided. The bench where David sat was nestled among an arrangement of wooden planters with low-growing evergreens and flowering shrubs. Beyond the windbreak the glass wall provided, lounge chairs were lined up along the deck, facing the railing. It was an "at sea" day today, as the ship made its way around the Italian peninsula to its next stop at Naples. Apart from a blue smudge of land on the horizon, all that was visible past the railing were the sun-dappled waves.

Marina stepped over his legs again and sat beside him. "Did Stefan have another nightmare last night?" she asked.

David shook his head. "He slept fine."

"That's good. Did he talk about any more monsters?"

"A little. He mentioned the one at the harbor again but he was okay once I promised I'd keep it away."

"He has a vivid imagination."

"Yes, and he's more willing to express himself now. I think this trip is helping him learn to handle his fears."

"Except for those nightmares, he is starting to act more like the child I remember, but that could be because I'm here, not because of the cruise. Seeing his family must make him feel more secure."

There was probably some truth in what she said, but David wasn't going to admit it and help make her case for her. He made a noncommittal noise.

She leaned to the side so she could see past him into the children's center. "It looks as if they're singing."

He turned his head to follow her gaze. "He appears to be having fun."

"Congratulations. You managed to schedule fun after all."

He faced her again. She was still leaning forward. The breeze caught a lock of her hair and teased it across the side of his chin.

So much for his relaxed pose. Her scent zinged through his senses. He half closed his eyes, tipping his face toward her hair to get more of the accidental caress....

Damn, he had to keep his mind on his priorities. He cleared his throat. "As long as Stefan's busy, I wanted to talk to you about something, Marina."

She pursed her lips. "I can tell I'm not going to like this. You're sounding too polite."

Her pucker distracted him for a second. He resolutely turned his gaze to the horizon. He wasn't making the progress with Marina that he'd hoped for. So far, they'd spent most of their time together sparring and not getting anywhere. He needed to try a different approach. "How long have you wanted to be a mother?"

"What?"

"My ex-wife and I had planned a family for years. I was eager to become a father, but I wanted to know when you started thinking about being a mother. You've never been married, have you?"

"No."

"Why not?"

She didn't reply, but he could hear when she twisted on the bench to face him. She was wearing her bracelets today, and the silver tinkled against the wooden bench as she leaned her arm on the back. The breeze caught a fold of her skirt, fluttering it against his leg.

He shoved his hands into his pockets so it wouldn't be as easy to reach for her. "I realize it's a personal question," he said, "but I believe it's relevant."

"I knew marriage wasn't for me from the first time I picked up a pencil and drew a wildflower."

"How's that?"

"To understand, you would have to see Murmansk in winter. It's...dark. I longed for color and beauty." She grasped her skirt and pressed it to the side of her leg.

David tried not to look at her thigh. "What did that have to do with staying single?"

"I felt a need to make beautiful things. It's why I began designing clothes. I started out by dyeing or altering Olena's hand-me-downs and learned I had a talent for it. My sister was content to stay where she was and be a fisherman's wife like our mother, but I wanted more. That's why I moved to Moscow to study design and pursued a career in fashion."

"Are you saying your career kept you too busy to consider marriage?"

She pursed her lips again. "If I say yes, you'll say that I would be too busy to be a parent, too. Is that where this is leading?"

"In a way. I realize how important it was to you to find Stefan, and how you really do care for him."

"I love him with all my heart."

"And I can see that he loves his aunt. I was just wondering whether you've really considered all the implications of becoming a parent."

"What implications? I love him, and he loves me. That's enough for any relationship. The details will sort themselves out later."

Marina's view of relationships was overly simplified and dead wrong. No commitment should be entered into solely on the basis of emotions. Love was never enough. There had to be planning and effort, clearheaded decisions and an ongoing desire to make the relationship work. The worst thing anyone could do was to take love for granted.

But love wasn't the topic David wanted to discuss. He took one hand from his pocket and touched Marina's elbow. "You'll always be Stefan's aunt, and he'll always be your nephew. I don't want to change that."

"You want to take him away from me."

"Marina, you never had him in the first place. You only visited him a few times a year. You told me you didn't need to see your family to feel their presence in your heart."

"I know I said that, but—"

"Would it make that much difference if you came to Burlington to visit him instead of going to Murmansk?"

She drew herself up. He could see she was about to launch into one of her tirades so he staved it off by moving his finger to her lips.

It wasn't a good idea. The feel of her mouth accelerated his pulse faster than any workout would have. He focused on where he touched her. She wasn't wearing lipstick—she must have been in too much of a hurry this morning to put on her makeup—so the rosy color was all hers. He pressed his thumb to her lower lip, absorbing the softness, enjoying the resilience, wondering how it would feel if he kissed her.

Her breath puffed across his finger. "You should take your hand away, David," she murmured.

He lifted his gaze. "You should move your head back, Marina."

She remained motionless. In spite of the sunshine, her

pupils were expanding, darkening her gaze even as her eyes narrowed in challenge.

In response, David trailed his thumb down her lower lip and touched her chin. He hadn't counted the number of times she'd touched him lately, but he hadn't forgotten a single one. Had she realized how it had affected him?

He didn't believe she'd done it deliberately to tease him, though. It was all part of the way she expressed herself. She was a passionate woman. She wasn't accustomed to restraint. What would it be like if she could channel that passion into something more enjoyable than arguing with him?

The image slammed through him without warning: Marina's pink skirt hiked to her waist, her long legs wrapped around his hips and the sun on his back. Her hair strewn across the wooden bench and her lips trembling against his…

David muttered an oath and dropped his hand. What the hell was the matter with him? That was the kind of fantasy one of his teenage students would have. He was a responsible, thirty-five-year-old man. A father. He should control his thoughts better than this.

Marina blinked, then slid to the other end of the bench, doubling the distance between them. Bracelets jangled as she crossed her arms. "I would never be satisfied with only that."

For a mad instant he thought she'd read his mind and shared the same fantasy. Well, he wouldn't be satisfied with a quick grapple on a bench, either. They would need privacy, a bed and at least a few hours, maybe a few nights….

He took a deep breath and forced his thoughts back on track. "Before you dismiss the idea of visiting us, think about it, all right? I've been preparing for years to raise a child. I have everything I need already in place. You would have to turn your life upside down in order to find ways to fit Stefan into it. Why not keep things the way they are?"

"Why not? Have you not listened to anything I've said these past four days?"

"All I'm asking is that you think about it." He gestured toward the room where Stefan played. "See how happy he is, even though you're not there? Sometimes the best way to show your love is to let go."

MARINA PACED ACROSS HER living room, the phone pressed to her ear. "I want you to do whatever is necessary, Rudolph. I don't care how much it costs me. Just stop that man from taking my nephew away."

"I'm working on it, Marina."

"We need something now. Surely there is some lawyer's trick you can do."

"What happened? Has he hurt Stefan?"

"No, of course not."

"We could try to get an emergency injunction if the child was in imminent danger."

"He isn't. David's wonderful with him."

"Then why the sudden urgency?"

She reversed direction and paced the other way. When she passed the love seat, she picked up the throw cushion with her free hand and hurled it against the wall. It hit with a muted sigh that was far from gratifying.

"Marina? I thought you were still hoping to change his mind."

"Yes, but it appears it's going to be harder than I thought. He's very…" She reached for the right word. Persuasive. Disarming. "Determined," she said. "He's determined and stubborn."

"And here I thought you two had nothing in common," he said dryly.

"We don't. David's stubbornness comes from his head, not his heart. He offered me visitation privileges. He thought I would be content with that."

"Actually, that was a smart move. It shows a willingness to compromise."

"It was an insult. How dare he throw me his scraps? He thinks he knows what's best. He lectures me like a teacher. He thinks I'm not a fit parent." She wiped her cheeks with her palm. "He said I could visit Vermont as often as I went to Murmansk. It's Olena all over again."

"I'm sure he didn't mean it as an insult."

"Whose side are you on, Rudolph?"

He paused. "You don't need to ask that."

Marina lifted her arm to blot her eyes on her sleeve. "Sorry. I know you'll come up with something. You have a very orderly mind."

"Thank you. There is one thing…"

"What?"

"Because of the spelling error in Stefan's name, the original documents Anderson and his lawyer arranged had to be amended."

"Yes, he said they were corrected."

"The more paperwork that was done, the more chance there would have been that additional errors could have arisen. Perhaps we could pursue that avenue for the time being rather than the adoption itself."

"I don't understand."

"If I could find even the smallest oversight in the paperwork that was filed, a sympathetic judge might deem it grounds to declare them invalid."

"Would that cancel the adoption?"

"Not the adoption, the travel documents."

"What would that mean?"

"If Stefan's travel documents were revoked, Anderson wouldn't be able to take your nephew to America with him."

Marina grasped the back of the love seat and stopped her pacing in midcircuit. "Then Stefan would have to return to Russia while it's sorted out, right?"

"Yes."

"Rudolph, that's deviously brilliant."

"It would only be a temporary solution, Marina. I can't promise it will happen, either, since there isn't much time left. And if Anderson decides to leave the cruise early and take Stefan directly home before I can pursue this, legally there would be nothing we could do."

"He wouldn't leave early. Stefan's enjoying himself, and David still believes he can change my mind."

"Then shall I go ahead?"

She wasn't sure why she hesitated. When David had agreed to discuss custody with her, they hadn't set any rules. This wasn't really underhanded. After all, *he'd* capitalized on a clerical error in order to take Stefan from *her.*

"Yes," she replied finally. "Go ahead, Rudolph. Do whatever it takes." She terminated the call and tossed the telephone receiver on the love seat, then flung herself into an armchair.

Sometimes the best way to show your love is to let go.

She slid down on her spine and thumped her head against the chair back. David had a knack for saying things that seemed to stick in her mind.

But that particular comment had been preposterous. Show her love for her nephew by letting go? That sounded like some convoluted feel-good babble from an American talk show host. What kind of woman would she be if she simply gave up? How could she possibly conceive of saying goodbye to her nephew? She'd stood up with him at his christening and vowed to take care of him. She was his only family. If she gave him up, she would be alone. If she let him go, she would prove that Olena had been right, that she wasn't meant to be a mother.

Marina thumped her head against the chair again. David was a very persuasive man. He also knew a lot about raising children.

But he was dead wrong about love. Love was too precious to simply let it go. She could understand why David might think some people would, since his birth mother had given up on him. He hadn't told Marina anything about his marriage, but she suspected his wife had been the one to call it quits rather than David. He took his commitments too seriously to be the one who did the leaving.

If Marina ever loved a man, she wouldn't let him go. She would follow him to the ends of the earth. She would hold him in her arms all night and in her thoughts all day. And she wouldn't need her art or her wealth to make their world beautiful as long as she could see those tiny lines beside his amber eyes crinkle and the sexy cowboy grooves beside his mouth deepen with his smile....

Marina slid from the chair to the floor and put her face in her hands.

This was why she'd asked Rudolph to pull out all the stops in her bid to get Stefan. The more time she spent with David, the more confused she got. He had a smile that could melt her resistance and a touch that could scatter her thoughts. It didn't seem to matter how often she warned herself to ignore the attraction, or how disloyal to Stefan it made her feel. It was getting stronger instead of going away.

It was loneliness, proximity, hormones, need, maybe even the holiday atmosphere. Except for her trips home, she never took vacations. Her work was her life. These days on the ship were giving her too much time on her hands. She shouldn't be surprised that David was having such an effect on her.

But it wasn't love. Definitely not love. Even Marina wasn't reckless enough to call it that.

ILYA FEDOROVICH SELDOM HAD cause to visit Naples. He didn't do business here—the criminal organizations in Italy were too well established and self-contained to hire an outsider—so the territory was unfamiliar to him. Yet he was confident the taxi driver hadn't been connected to the local *camorra,* because the man had shown far more curiosity than had been wise.

It hadn't been any of the driver's business why Ilya had told him to follow the tour bus from the harbor through the streets of Naples, or why he should wait while the passengers went to lunch. He shouldn't have asked why Ilya had him park so they could see the couple with the blond child, or why he'd been told to drive on when the local police had passed by. No, a man who was imprudent enough to ask questions like that couldn't have had mob connections. And even if he had, he'd been too foolish to be anyone significant so there wouldn't be repercussions. Ilya checked the alley once more to ensure he was still unobserved, then opened the door and rolled the driver's corpse out of the car.

Not a twinge of regret troubled Ilya's mind. He'd given the man an easier death than most of the other deaths that could have been in store for him. Every person in the world was born to die. Ilya merely had determined when.

He spat on the pavement to cleanse the bloody saliva from his mouth, adjusted the seat to accommodate his long legs, then drove out of the alley to the square where the tour bus was parked. Only another three hours remained before the ship was scheduled to leave Naples. He wanted to wrap this up today—he had other jobs waiting for him in Moscow. It was already taking far longer than he'd planned.

In spite of Misha's failure to get him on *Alexandra's Dream*, Ilya had come close to finishing the hit two days ago in Dubrovnik. He'd spotted the couple with the Gorsky child when they'd disembarked from the ship, but he had lost track of them once they'd started criss-crossing the city in taxis. He hadn't seen them again until they'd returned to the harbor. He would have made his move then if it hadn't been for the pair of policemen who had chosen that moment to walk from the ship to their car.

Ilya suspected the boy had recognized him, given his reaction when he'd spotted Ilya at the pier. That was one complication he hadn't anticipated. The number of tourists with cameras who surrounded the boy today was another. Anderson and the Artamova woman had remained with the tour group since they'd left the Naples harbor, so Ilya had been forced to stay out of sight as he waited for an opportunity to present itself.

He turned up the collar of his black shirt and stroked his cheek with the backs of his fingers. Killing the taxi driver had dulled the ache, but it would return. It always did. Frowning, he scanned the square until he spotted the boy. He was walking along the edge of the fountain, his hand clasped in his aunt's. She was dressed in bright purple

today and easier to spot than the boy. By contrast, except
for his height, the beige-clad Anderson didn't stand out in
a crowd. Artamova and Anderson made an odd couple, but
they'd been united in their unrelenting vigilance of the
Gorsky boy.

Ilya's own parents had coddled him almost as badly.
They hadn't done him any favor. They had been too weak
to prepare him for the realities of survival and had left him
defenseless. Easy prey. He hadn't learned how poorly
they'd served him until he'd been sent to the front at
eighteen. His first kill had been a revelation. That was when
the rules he'd been raised by had proven to be irrelevant.
It was the army that had taught him the true meaning of life
was the ability to dispense death. In the mountains of Afghanistan, he'd learned how to be the hunter, not the prey.

The Gorsky boy jumped off the rim of the fountain and
clapped his hands, a carefree fool of a child who didn't
know what was coming. Ilya's fingers drummed on the
steering wheel. All he needed was one unguarded moment,
an instant when they were separated from the crowd, but
he could see the tour group was starting to gather at the bus.
Anderson took Artamova's elbow and was obviously trying
to guide her toward the others, but she shook her head and
gestured toward the boy.

Ilya's lips curved. It was clear by their body language
that the two adults were quarreling. It wasn't the first time
he'd noticed that today. Good. Arguing would distract them
from the child.

Artamova was pointing to one of the shops on the ground
floor of the building across the road. It had a large plastic ice
cream cone beside the door. Ilya slid his hand into his pocket
and fingered his gun. They might take their gazes off the

child if they ordered ice cream. The late afternoon sunshine didn't penetrate the open archway that made up the front of the shop, so if he pulled the trigger as he walked past…

There! The boy's aunt had turned her back on Anderson and was heading for the street on her own with the boy. This was the first time the child hadn't been flanked by the two of them when he walked. Ilya rapidly assessed his options. This was too good an opportunity to pass up. And how fitting it would be if he finished the Gorsky job as he'd started it. The taxi wasn't as heavy a vehicle as the sedan he'd used in Murmansk, but he'd be using it against a child, not a car, so it would be more than adequate.

He jammed the gas pedal to the floor. The tires squealed as he left the curb and hurtled toward the crosswalk. The woman was looking the other way and didn't see him coming, but the child did. For a split second he looked straight through the windshield at Ilya's face.

Power surged through Ilya's veins as he saw the horror in the boy's gaze. His teeth closed on his scar and he tasted blood in his mouth once more. The familiar red haze clouded the edges of his vision, tightening his focus. He trembled on the edge of release. Yes. At last.

Yet the instant before Ilya would have crushed the boy beneath his wheels, Anderson appeared out of nowhere. He leaped in front of the car to shove the woman and child out of the way.

Ilya swerved to correct his course, but the car was going too fast for him to change direction far enough.

Instead of hitting the boy, he hit the man.

CHAPTER SEVEN

"WHAT'S TAKING SO long?" Marina demanded. "The paramedics checked him over before they brought him back to the ship. Did you find something else wrong? Is there some problem they missed?"

The nurse squeezed Marina's shoulder and steered her toward the padded bench in the reception room. "Relax, Mrs. Anderson. Your husband is in remarkably good condition, considering what he went through. He's a lucky man. We're just giving him a thorough examination to make sure we can handle his needs before we leave the harbor."

"He's not my husband," Marina said. "We're just…" She paused. She'd run into this issue at least a dozen times over the past few hours, both in English and Italian, but she hadn't yet settled on a good word to describe what David was to her. "When can we see him?" she asked.

"It shouldn't be long now. The doctor will be out to speak with you shortly. Please, have a seat."

The medical center on *Alexandra's Dream* was compact but was reputed to be fully equipped and prepared to handle any emergency. The staff appeared well-trained, exuding the perfect mixture of competence and reassurance. The paramedics who had treated David at the scene had deemed his injuries were minor, some scrapes and bruises and a sprained knee, since the car hadn't hit him head-on. He didn't require hospitalization, but Marina couldn't believe he'd gotten off that lightly. Glancing blow or not, he'd been hit by a car. God, she could still hear the thud.

She glanced at the bench and then at the doors to the treatment area. If she had been on her own, she would have ignored the nurse and already pushed her way through those doors to verify David's condition for herself, but she had to think of what was best for Stefan.

He hadn't spoken a word since the hit-and-run. Instead he'd been sucking his thumb. The only sounds he'd made were hiccups and sobs. The incident must have stirred horrible memories for him. He didn't need to be alarmed further.

She sat on the bench, pulled Stefan onto her lap and buried her nose in his hair. This was her fault. She never should have dragged him across the road for that ice cream. She should have paid closer attention to her surroundings. She should have noticed that crazy driver.

But she hadn't. And now David was hurt and Stefan was traumatized, and all because she'd been annoyed with David over their boring tour. No, it had been more than that. She'd wanted to prove she could entertain Stefan better than David could. And she'd wanted to put some distance between her and that devastating smile of his.

And David had repaid her pettiness by saving her life.

What if he hadn't pushed them aside in time? What if that driver had hit Stefan instead? She and David were so busy arguing about who got custody of this child, but what if there was no child…?

She shuddered, unable to complete the thought. Stefan was unhurt. He was fine. She could feel the warmth of his small frame and smell the little-boy sweetness of his scalp. For his sake, she had to try to be calm. "Hey, Stefochka," she said, rocking him back and forth. "Do you remember the song the birds on the box sang?"

He tipped his face to look at her. The skin around his eyes was mottled with red from his crying but it appeared his tears had stopped.

Marina smiled and hummed a few bars of "Lara's Theme," the tune from the music box she'd given Stefan. But it was probably not the best choice since it was so sad. Why else would her own eyes be filling with tears?

"Mrs. Anderson?"

At the male voice, she looked up quickly. The man who stood in front of her was wearing the uniform of a ship's officer, not that of a doctor. "I'm Marina Artamova," she said. "Mr. Anderson's…" *What? Opponent? Admirer? Friend?* "Acquaintance," she finished.

The man dipped his chin to acknowledge the correction. He was a handsome man, not as tall as David, yet he appeared just as solidly built and carried himself with the balanced grace of an athlete. "I'm Gideon Dayan," he said, extending his hand. "Chief of Security for *Alexandra's Dream.*"

She shook his hand. "Have they caught the hit-and-run driver yet?"

"I've just finished speaking with the Naples police. They found the vehicle a few blocks from the accident scene but there was no trace of the driver."

She'd already been questioned by the police, but she hadn't been able to give them much information. She hadn't seen anything until she'd heard Stefan cry out and felt David shove them. "It was a taxi."

"Yes, they're searching for the owner now."

"Whoever it is should be locked up. They're a menace. If it hadn't been for David—" Her voice broke. She couldn't complete the thought now, either. She pressed her lips together and hugged Stefan.

"I've asked the Naples authorities to keep me informed while they continue to investigate the accident."

"They will be able to arrest the person when they find him, won't they? Even though we came back to the ship?"

"Yes. They have your statements, as well as the accounts of several other tourists who were in the area."

"Good."

"If you remember any more details, or if you would like an update on the investigation's progress, please feel free to contact me."

"I will."

"In the meantime, if there's anything we can do to make you more comfortable, just let us know."

"Thank you, but what I'd really like is to know how Mr. Anderson is—" She broke off when she saw one of the doors to the treatment area swing open. The man who came through wasn't a doctor, it was David.

A large square of white gauze was taped across his forehead. More gauze circled his right forearm below the elbow. The ripped, bloodstained golf shirt and beige Dockers he'd been wearing when he was brought here had been replaced by a set of clean clothes. His face and hands were clean, too. Apart from his bandages and the crutches that he held under his arms, he looked almost normal.

Before she could stand, Stefan wriggled off her lap and raced across the reception room. He wrapped both arms around David's right leg.

David's face blanched. He reached down with one hand

to shift Stefan to his other leg, then ruffled his hair un-steadily. "Hey, there, champ. You must be hungry. What do you say we get some pizza?"

Marina had been wrong. He didn't look normal. She could see the lines of strain around his eyes. The skin beside his lips was pinched white with pain. He obviously shouldn't be on his feet so soon. What on earth was he thinking?

But then she saw the smile on Stefan's face and realized what David had done. Of course. He hadn't wanted to worry Stefan with his appearance. That's why he'd found a way to change clothes, and had mustered the strength to move under his own power. It was probably why he'd insisted on being brought back to the ship, too, so that Stefan would be in a more familiar environment.

She wiped her eyes with the heels of her hands and walked to where David stood with her nephew. Close up, she could see a scrape on David's right cheekbone that hadn't been bandaged. She hated to imagine the bruises that were coming up beneath his clean clothes. He belonged in bed. What a ridiculously stubborn man. He was probably in agony. So she was careful to keep her touch featherlight as she cupped his face in her palms and stretched up to kiss him.

She hadn't planned to kiss him. She'd thought about it often enough, but never would she have anticipated doing it under circumstances like these.

Yet there were no words in any of the languages she knew that could express how she felt at this moment. Only a kiss would do.

It started out gently because her lips were trembling too badly for her to make a solid connection. She tried to remember his injuries and be considerate of his condition, but then she felt his mouth move against hers and she rose up on her toes to press closer.

He kissed the way he smiled. No, not his polite, hiding-his-feelings smiles but one of the real smiles, the kind that let her glimpse the passion he kept so tightly controlled. His lips were supple, slanting across hers as he tilted his head to find a better fit. His breath warmed her cheek. The tip of his tongue teased the seam of her lips.

"Dad! Aunt Nina!"

At Stefan's voice, Marina snapped her eyes open. She drew back her head and blinked to bring David's face into focus. And she still couldn't think of a word to say.

Apparently neither could he. He inhaled slowly, his nostrils flaring. His lips were still parted. Gold flecks she hadn't noticed before sparkled in his amber gaze.

She ran a fingertip beside the scrape on his cheek. The evidence of what had happened to him didn't make her want to stop, it only made her want to kiss him again.

"Monster! See monster."

They both looked down at Stefan. He was still hanging on to David's leg with one arm and had grabbed Marina's skirt with his other hand. His chin was quivering, as if he were about to start crying again.

"It's all right, son," David said. His voice was hoarse. He cleared his throat. "There aren't any monsters now. I'll keep you safe, I promise."

Stefan stamped his foot and looked at Marina. He switched to Russian, talking as quickly as he had when he'd told her about his nightmare. He described the same ogre as before, the one with the pale, scarred face and the black wings.

But this time he hadn't seen it in his nightmare or on a dock, he'd seen it driving the car that had hit David.

DAVID NODDED HIS thanks as Gideon handed him the glass of water. He shook out one of the pills the ship's doctor had given him, downed it with the water, then returned the pill bottle to his pants pocket. He'd held off on the medication as long as he could because he'd wanted to keep a clear head, but the pain was starting to win. "I appreciate your meeting me so late, Mr. Dayan."

"We could postpone this until tomorrow," Gideon said, placing the water glass on his desk. "You look like you could use some rest."

David shifted on the chair, trying to find a more comfortable position, yet until the medication hit his system nothing would help. His right side had received most of the damage, and every square inch was reminding him of his collision with the taxi's fender and the pavement. He'd rather be in bed, but he had to make use of this opportunity while his son was asleep to meet Gideon in private. Although Marina didn't agree with what he was doing, she was watching Stefan until he returned. "No, I'd prefer to talk to you now. I'll keep this brief."

Gideon sat behind his desk, opened the file folder that lay on top of it and uncapped his pen. His office was small and windowless, a room designed for function rather than appearance. David was sure the state-of-the-art electronics that lined the shelves along the walls were only the tip of the iceberg as far as the ship's security system went. "Go ahead," Gideon said. "I'll relay your information to the Naples police."

"This isn't about today's accident. It's about an unrelated matter."

"All right. How can I help you?"

"This concerns my adopted son, Stefan. You met him earlier today."

"Yes, I remember. The little Russian boy."

David regarded the security chief. Gideon struck him as a competent man, in spite of his film-star good looks. It remained to be seen whether or not he would take David's worries seriously. This wasn't going to be an easy sell—David wasn't totally convinced himself—but he had to try. "I'm concerned that Stefan either witnessed abuse at one of the orphanages where he was staying, or someone there mistreated him."

Gideon immediately sat forward. "Do you wish to have him examined by our medical staff?"

This was one of the toughest questions David had already asked himself. He tried to answer as calmly as he could, even though the very idea made him feel sick to his stomach. "I don't think that would do Stefan any good at this point. He has no recent or unexplained injuries. He's not afraid of being touched, either, so he doesn't behave like a child who has been sexually assaulted. If it turns out he does need professional help I'll arrange a specialist when I get home."

"If he has no physical injuries, why do you suspect abuse? Did he tell you about it?"

"No."

"Then—"

"He's had nightmares about a monster. He imagined he saw the same monster driving the car that hit me. That's why he was so agitated when you met him."

"He imagines monsters," Gideon said slowly. "I see."

David persevered despite the skepticism in Gideon's voice. "His description of this monster is very vivid and specific, which is why I believe he could be describing an actual person."

"You think the monster in his nightmare could in fact be someone from the orphanage."

"Yes, I do. Stefan had a happy life before his parents died and he was sent there. It must be the source of his anxiety."

Gideon tapped his pen against the desktop. "Or it could be just a bad dream."

David shook his head, then gritted his teeth against the wave of dizziness that followed. "That's what I believed the first time it happened. I thought it was only an isolated incident, but this is becoming a pattern. I can't ignore the possibility that my son is trying to tell me something."

"By talking about a monster?"

"Yes. There aren't many avenues of communication open to a child when they are afraid of an adult, especially an adult who is a caregiver. No one wants to believe them, because none of us want to admit that monsters really do exist."

"I understand, but—"

"No, I don't think you do understand, Mr. Dayan. All it takes for an abuser to go unpunished is for one person to dismiss a child's fears."

"Children have active imaginations."

"Sure, they do. They make things up all the time. That doesn't mean they make everything up. Whatever the reason, my son is terrified of a tall man with a scar."

Gideon replaced the cap on his pen and stood. "I'm not sure what you think I can do for you or your son, Mr. Anderson. I oversee the security aboard *Alexandra's Dream*. My authority doesn't extend past this ship."

David reached for his crutches, levered himself out of his chair and swung himself forward to face Gideon across his desk. "You can contact the people who do have authority, can't you?"

"What do you have in mind?"

"Stefan was at orphanages in St. Petersburg and in Murmansk. Contact the police in those cities. Ask them to check the staff at those orphanages for a tall, pasty-faced man who likes to wear black and who has a scar shaped like a sickle on his cheek. Maybe he works there. Maybe he only visits. Maybe he *is* nothing but a figment of my son's imagination, but if he does exist, he should be investigated."

"On the basis of your son's dreams?"

"I realize how this sounds, yet it wouldn't hurt to make a few phone calls, would it?"

"Mr. Anderson, I can see you're sincere, but frankly it would be a waste of time to approach the police without something more substantial to go on."

"Damn it, what have you got to lose? Either you'll all have a good laugh at an overzealous new parent, or you'll stop a monster who is abusing defenseless orphans." David halted, his throat suddenly dry. He had to swallow before he could continue. "Whatever happened to Stefan in the past, he's safe now. I'll always protect him. But who's going to protect the children who are left?"

Gideon appeared to mull that over for a while, then nodded curtly. "Give me the phone numbers of those orphanages. I'll make some inquiries myself."

The offer wasn't nearly as much as he'd hoped for, but David could see by Gideon's expression it was all he was going to get. He gripped his crutches more tightly, bracing himself against a wave of pain. His knee was aching and his bruises were throbbing, yet not all of the pain came from his injuries. Some came from his memories.

He'd sensed from the beginning that he and Stefan shared a bond. He needed to make sure it wasn't *this* deep. "Thank you, Mr. Dayan. I just hope to God I'm wrong."

"So do I, Mr. Anderson."

EVEN IN MAY, THE Mediterranean sunlight had a pure, piercing quality unlike anywhere else in the world. It had heated the deck quickly, gleaming from the polished railings and sparkling from the water in the pool. People sipped drinks at umbrella-shaded tables while determined tanners were baking themselves on lounge chairs. Swimmers dunked and splashed—the pool where Marina floated was for relaxing, not for doing laps—yet overall, the area wasn't as busy as it usually was.

The ship had arrived at Civitavecchia, the port that served Rome, early this morning. Most of the passengers were taking full advantage of the opportunity to go ashore and visit what was known around the world as the Eternal City. Marina had traveled to Rome often and had been looking forward to showing Stefan the postcard-famous landmarks, as well as places that weren't on any tour. There was her favorite gelato bar with stools shaped like rearing horses. And there was a pasta shop where the window display always featured an array of whimsical creatures fashioned from different types of pasta. Glimpses of history and feasts for the senses waited around every corner.

But David was in no shape to go anywhere, and he wouldn't have allowed her to take Stefan touring without him. Not that she'd asked. It wouldn't have been fair to take advantage of his condition in order to further her cause with Stefan. Besides, David was in a foul mood today, which was to be expected since he was trying to be stoic about his discomfort. Marina readily admitted that if she had been the one who'd been struck by a car, she wouldn't be suffering in silence.

She pulled herself out of the pool, toweled herself off and fastened her cover-up wrap skirt over her bathing suit. Then she dragged a lounge chair next to David's so she would have a better view of the Plexiglass-fenced area next to the railing that enclosed the children's wading pool. "Stefan's subdued this afternoon," she said.

"He's still shaken up." David adjusted his sunglasses. "He needs to realize he's safe."

She watched her nephew splash around the edge of the pool. He was with a group of kids led by Gemma Slater, the girl who worked in the children's program. They were playing a game that involved shoving a huge, blue-and-white beach ball across the surface of the water. When it went to Stefan, though, he missed because he was looking at David and Marina instead of the ball. He'd been checking on them frequently while he played, as if he wanted to reassure himself they were still there.

"I think the accident yesterday might have made him remember the one that killed Olena and Borya," she said.

"It could have."

"Has he talked about it to you?"

"No."

"What should we do if he does?"

"We'll let him talk. It's healthy. That way he'll be in control of the memories and can get over them."

Marina chewed her lip. David believed the monster from Stefan's nightmares was a memory, too. In fact, he'd taken her nephew's description seriously enough to talk to the ship's security chief about it. That had surprised her.

David had seemed far too rational and levelheaded to do something like asking the authorities to investigate a nightmare.

She suspected the main reason David thought Stefan's monster might be real was that he didn't want to accept the more obvious explanation for Stefan's fears. A car accident had killed Stefan's parents, so seeing another accident would have to remind him of all he'd lost. There had been too many changes in his life, and no matter how well-intentioned David's adoption of him was, her nephew was bound to be missing his home, his language, his culture and his family. The nightmare ogre was just Stefan's way of giving his anxieties a face.

But she and David had already gone over this, and she wouldn't feel right about using it to score points. She wasn't going to harp on the fact that his actions could be at the root of what was upsetting Stefan, especially after what had happened yesterday. David hadn't yet spoken a word of blame, even though they both knew that she was the one who had decided to cross the road in spite of the traffic.

She glanced at the crutches that he'd left on the deck beside his chair. Along with one of his typical off-white cotton shirts, he was wearing shorts instead of pants today, so she was able to see the elastic bandage wrapped around his sprained knee. He'd replaced the gauze square on his forehead with a smaller, less noticeable bandage that was partly hidden by the ends of his hair, but a purple bruise had appeared along the edges of the scrape on his cheek.

"David? About yesterday…"

He turned his head. His eyes were hidden behind the dark lenses of his sunglasses, but he couldn't conceal the tension in the firm set of his jaw. "Yes?"

"I wanted to thank you," she said.

"Why?"

"For saving my life."

"You're welcome." He turned his head back toward the pool. "I was also saving Stefan's," he added.

"Yes, I realize that."

"Is that why you kissed me?"

She should have known they wouldn't be able to avoid the subject forever. That kiss had been hovering between them with the same intensity as one of those memorable comments David was so good at making.

Oh, she wanted to lie. It would be easy to claim she'd only kissed him out of gratitude, but it wasn't as simple as that. She studied his profile. He was looking more like a cowboy than ever today. It was probably because of the scraped cheekbone. It gave him an air of toughness.

"Why did you kiss me, Marina?" he asked.

She put on her own sunglasses and stretched out on her chair. "Because I felt like it."

"You were distraught."

"Deh."

"I think you mean 'duh.'"

"Fine. Duh. Of course I was distraught. You could have been killed."

"That would have solved the issue of custody for you."

She sat up quickly and swung her feet to the deck between them. She'd tried to be patient with his mood, but he seemed to be deliberately goading her. "How dare you make light of what happened? And how could you imply I would want to see you hurt? I might want to smack you now and then because you are a truly maddening man at times but I would never wish you harm."

"So you kissed me because you were distraught and grateful?"

"Well, it certainly wasn't because I was overcome with desire. You looked terrible. You still do. You look as if…"

"As if I was hit by a car?"

"I said don't make light of it. I saw how you swayed on your feet when you got here. You were ready to collapse by the time you sat down. You should have asked for a wheelchair instead of using those crutches."

"I'm accustomed to getting around on crutches. I wrecked the same knee two years ago playing soccer."

"And don't think I missed how you winced when you leaned back on that chair. You must be covered in bruises."

"Not that many more than I have after playing football with my brothers. It doesn't hurt as much as yesterday. I look worse than I feel."

"That's impossible. You should have gone home instead of insisting on continuing your holiday…." She caught herself before she could expand on that. What was she thinking? If David took Stefan home early, she wouldn't be able to see either of them. Worse, Rudolph wouldn't have the opportunity to work on revoking Stefan's travel documents.

Her conscience twinged at that, but she told herself to ignore it. The fact that Stefan was still seeing his nightmare monster only proved how wrong the adoption was. He belonged in his native country with his aunt.

"I can recuperate on the ship more easily than at home," David said. "There's no maid or room service at my house, and besides, I've already paid for this cruise."

"You're just being heroic because you don't want to upset Stefan by showing him you're hurt."

"Heroic?" He snorted. "I'm just an ordinary school-teacher from Vermont, Marina."

Five days ago she'd thought the same thing. She'd believed he was bland and boring, and she'd been completely wrong. Every day, he revealed another facet of his strength, and it wasn't only physical.

Still, she couldn't discount the physical. Her gaze strayed from his bandaged knee to his good leg. She'd never found a man's legs particularly attractive, but David's could change her opinion about that. Even at rest, the muscles of his thighs and calves were well-defined, no doubt a side effect of the soccer and football he played.

"Do you have a boyfriend waiting for you back in Moscow?" he asked.

"Why?"

"You said that marriage wasn't for you, but that doesn't rule out having a man in your life. How would he fit into your plan to raise Stefan?"

She sighed. It appeared they were back to scoring points, after all. "There is no boyfriend."

"That's hard to believe. I would have thought a woman of your temperament would have a string of admirers."

This time she was the one who snorted. "It has been my experience that a woman's temperament is the last thing men are interested in. I've never had any man try to grope my temperament."

"Then what do they try to grope?"

"Usually my purse or my checkbook."

"I find that hard to believe, Marina."

"I happen to be exceedingly gifted in the checkbook department, David."

"A checkbook won't keep anyone warm at night."

"Paying one's fuel bills does, and it eliminates the need to fight over the blankets. I enjoy my independence and have little use for men."

"If that's how you feel, obviously you've tried kissing the wrong ones."

"I agree. It seems lately that I have chosen the wrong ones to kiss."

"Well, you won't have any shortage of choice if you keep flaunting yourself in that outfit."

She glanced down at her bathing suit. It was a sample from her new beachwear line, and like all her designs, it was cut to flatter a real woman, not a runway model. Because of that, it contained more fabric than the bikinis that many of the other women around the pool were wearing. Granted, her wrap skirt had fallen back from her thighs when she'd twisted to face David, and the gold shirring across her midriff had drooped from her dip in the water. The way she was leaning toward David had brought her breasts dangerously close to spilling out of the top. She tugged at the straps to ease them more securely into place. "You're using your schoolteacher tone again and it's very annoying. This outfit is an Artamova original and will probably make me another fortune."

"Undoubtedly. Many men would pay a considerable amount for that view."

"And if you're going to imply next that I have loose morals just because I am comfortable with my body—"

"Smile."

"What?"

"Smile. Stefan's watching us and is looking worried."

She glanced toward the wading pool. He was right. Stefan was sucking hard on his thumb and had drawn his eyebrows together as he regarded her and David. She smiled and waggled her fingers at him as she spoke to David through her teeth. "My love life and my wardrobe have nothing to do with my ability to raise my nephew. He will always be my priority. And if you're trying to make a point against me because I kissed you, remember you did kiss me back."

"Yes, I did."

"Why? Was that for Stefan's benefit to pretend we were getting along?"

"What do you think?"

She swung her legs onto the chair again, flipped her skirt over her thighs, then leaned back and clasped her hands over her stomach. "The truth is, I didn't think, David. Not everything in life has to be analyzed or scheduled or *mean* something. It was just a kiss. God, you're annoying."

"Yes, you've mentioned that."

"Is that why your wife left you?"

The moment the question left her lips, she wanted to call it back. Sparring with David had made her momentarily forget his condition. She should be making allowances for his bad mood instead of aggravating it. She extended her arm across the space between their chairs and touched his knuckles. "I'm sorry," she said. "That wasn't fair."

He rolled his head along the back of the chair and regarded her, the expression in his eyes still veiled by his sunglasses. "I had it coming. I've been provoking you."

"I'll signal a steward for some water. You must be due for another pain pill."

He grasped her hand before she could raise her arm. "I think I can go a round with you without medication."

His grip was strong, in spite of the bandage that wrapped

his upper forearm. She relaxed her hand rather than trying to yank it away. "David—"

"To be honest, I admire the way you don't let anyone push you around, Marina. You give as good as you get."

"I've heard it put in much less flattering terms."

"I'm sure you have. You're not an easy opponent."

"Believe it or not, I've been trying to maintain a truce with you today. You don't have to talk about your marriage if you don't want."

"Talking is all I'm capable of doing right now." He squeezed her fingers and released her hand. "What makes you think that my wife was the one who left?"

"Because I've seen how you are with Stefan. I don't believe you'd break your word easily."

"Well, you're right. Ellie was the one who left me."

"Didn't she want Stefan?"

"Yes, but not enough to stay."

A thought suddenly occurred to her. "She's not planning to be part of Stefan's life anyway, is she?"

"No. She's living in Boston now with her lover. They're getting married in the fall."

"That was fast."

"She had been seeing him for more than a year when she first suggested we try adoption. I'd thought she was trying to mend our marriage, but she was hedging her bets."

"What do you mean?"

"She'd been told by fertility specialists that she had little chance of conceiving, but she knew it was still possible." His jaw tightened. "Ellie had suggested adoption only to distract me. She'd planned to leave me for her boyfriend all along, but she delayed because she was trying to get pregnant by both of us."

Marina was stunned. What an incredible betrayal of trust. David's ex-wife clearly hadn't cared about anyone's feelings but her own. Being unfaithful was bad enough, but using David only as a potential sperm donor was reprehensible. "That's despicable. How could any woman do that to the man she'd vowed to love? I'm glad she left you. And I hope she never conceives a child. A woman that selfish would make a terrible mother."

"Funny. I used to think Ellie would make the perfect mother."

"Why? What was she like?"

He paused. "Nothing like you, Marina."

She wasn't sure how to take that. She already knew that David thought her far from ideal as a parent, yet she was pleased he didn't think she was like his ex-wife.

What an idiot that woman must have been. How could she have looked for love elsewhere when she'd had a strong, intelligent and sensitive man like David at home? She must have let her desire to have a child blind her to the love that David could have given her. Marina had known him less than a week, but she could plainly see that all the qualities that would make him a good father would also make him a wonderful husband....

Marina pressed back in her chair, shaken by what she'd just thought. *Husband?* That was the last thing she wanted. She'd meant what she'd told him. She enjoyed her independence and her work—there was no place in her life for a man. "You never answered my question," she said.

"Ellie left me because she was tired of me. Bored. Disinterested. Weary. Annoyed. Pick one."

"That wasn't the question I meant."

"Okay, what was your question?"

"Why did you kiss me back?"

He tipped down his sunglasses and looked at her over the edge of the frames. "Are you sure you want me to answer that?"

Marina caught her breath. The darkened skin around his eyes bore testament to how poorly he must have slept the night before. Yet the turmoil in his gaze was from more than just physical pain. Was it because she'd brought up the topic of his marriage? Was he still in love with Ellie?

Oh, she hoped not. David deserved better than that. He needed a woman who could coax his passion to the surface, not make him want to lock it up.

"Mr. Anderson?"

She started at the soft voice—she'd been too focused on David to notice anyone approaching. She looked up to see a tall, dark-haired woman standing at the foot of David's chair. It was Ariana Bennett, the ship's librarian.

"Hello, Ariana," David said, pushing his sunglasses back into place on his nose. "How are you today?"

"That was what I came to ask you," she said. She laced her fingers in front of her, as if she didn't know what to do without books in her arms. "I'm sorry I didn't come sooner, but I've been on duty. I wanted to tell you how horrified I was by what happened. I hope you're on the mend."

"The doctor says I'll be good as new in a few days."

Marina looked pointedly at his bandages, but she stopped herself from contradicting him. Considering David's stubbornness, he might fulfil the prediction.

"I'm amazed you weren't hurt worse," Ariana said. "That taxi didn't slow down at all."

"You sound as if you saw the accident," Marina said.

"Yes, I did," she replied. "I was on the far side of the fountain when I saw Mr. Anderson sprint for the crosswalk."

"I didn't see you with our tour group," David said.

"No, I wasn't on the tour. I, um—" She hesitated, lacing and unlacing her hands. "I wanted to explore Naples on my own. I'd never been there before, but I had lost my way. I was trying to hail that taxi but he passed me by without stopping." She glanced over her shoulder at the wading pool where Stefan played. "It all happened so fast. If you hadn't pushed your son out of the way…"

"Hang on," David said. "If you were going to hail that taxi, you must have been close enough to have seen the driver."

"Yes, but only for a few seconds. I already described him to the Naples police."

"Good," Marina said. "I hope they can identify him. That driver belongs behind bars."

"He shouldn't be that hard to find, considering his awful scar."

Marina felt as if she'd just been punched. She struggled for air. "Scar?"

David sat forward fast. "Did you say he had a *scar?*"

Ariana nodded and pointed to her cheek. "Yes, right here. It was lumpy and shaped in a crescent."

CHAPTER EIGHT

ARIANA BENNETT LOOKED at the couple in front of her, bewildered by their reactions. Marina's jaw had dropped and the color had drained from her face. Pressing her hand over her mouth, she muttered something in what sounded like Russian as she stared at her nephew. David swore and reached beside his chair to grab his crutches from the deck.

"I'm sorry," Ariana said. "I didn't mean to upset you by bringing this up. As I said, I did give a full statement to the police."

But it had been a belated statement, Ariana admitted to herself, given over the phone to a harried-sounding officer once she'd returned to the pier later that evening. She hadn't wanted to remain at the accident scene long enough to speak with the police in person because she'd had only a few hours left before the ship sailed and had still hoped to find the address she'd been seeking.

But she'd failed to locate it anyway. She hoped she hadn't made an error when she'd transcribed her father's notebook and loaded the data into her iPod. Either way, she would have to wait until the ship stopped in Naples on the next sailing to try again.

David twisted sideways on the lounge chair, angled a crutch under one of his arms and levered himself to his feet.

"Don't apologize," he said. "I want to thank you for letting us know. What else can you tell us about this scarred man?"

"I only saw him for a moment."

"That's more than I did," Marina said, shoving herself out of her chair. She grasped Ariana's arm. "Think back. What did he look like? What was he wearing?"

"His head was almost to the top of the cab, so he had to have been a tall man. And he was wearing black. A shirt, I think, because the collar was turned up."

"Damn!" David planted the tips of his crutches on the deck and swung himself toward the wading pool. "I should have believed him."

"You did," Marina said.

"Not about this. He told us the monster was in the car. I dismissed that completely."

Marina let go of Ariana and followed David toward the group Gemma was supervising. "But it doesn't make sense," Marina said. "How could Stefan have seen him before?"

The rest of their conversation was lost to Ariana as David and Marina reached Stefan. They both put on smiles for the child's benefit, but their tension was obvious as they dried him off and ushered him away from the pool.

What on earth had that been about? Ariana wondered. Had David actually said *monster?*

"Hello, Ariana. If you're going ashore, I'd be happy to show you around."

She gave an inward sigh as she recognized the voice of the first officer. Giorgio Tzekas had made it plain he was interested in her, and he likely thought she should be flattered by his attention.

But she hadn't taken this position on *Alexandra's Dream* in order to meet men. Romance was the furthest thing from her mind. That wasn't why she'd quit her job at the university and traveled halfway around the world. She was here because the name of this ship had been listed in her father's notebook, as had a series of addresses near Mediterranean ports. Either the ship or one of those addresses had to hold a clue as to what Derek Bennett had been up to before he'd died.

Ariana intended to prove that the FBI was wrong. Derek hadn't been a criminal, he'd been a dedicated museum curator. There was no way the father she had adored, and who had shared his own love of Greek and Roman history with his only daughter, could have done what the police had claimed.

No, it was all a mistake. Her father had studied and cataloged priceless artifacts. He couldn't possibly have been involved in a plot to smuggle them.

"TELL MR. DAYAN TO call me when he's free," David said. He gave the number of Marina's stateroom, slammed the phone on the dining table and returned his hand to his crutch.

Marina combed her hair with her fingers as she padded toward the table. She had changed from her bathing suit into a lemon yellow tunic and matching pants but her feet were still bare so the hems of her pant legs dragged on the carpet. "I assume the security chief is busy?" she asked.

"Either that, or he doesn't want to take my call."

"Now that I've had the chance to think about it, I have to wonder whether it's only coincidence, after all," Marina said, putting her palm on his back. "Just because Stefan dreamed about someone with a scar doesn't mean he dreamed about that particular man."

"The scar was the same shape."

"We only know it was curved, that's all. The man was probably just a Naples taxi driver, a bad driver, who got that scar in some other accident."

David curled his fingers around the crutch grip. "Come on, Marina. He was tall. He was wearing black. That's too many coincidences."

"Not really. There must be many tall men who dress in black. That's what frightened Stefan at the pier in Dubrovnik."

David felt as if the room was closing in on him. He swung away from Marina's touch and moved to the living room. "It must have been the same man. He must be following us from port to port."

"What? No, David, that's crazy."

"He's worried that Stefan is going to tell us what he did. He must have been following us since we left the orphanage."

"David—"

"He meant to hit us. Ariana said he didn't slow down. He must have been watching us and waiting for a chance…" David stopped and looked at the door to Marina's bedroom where Stefan was having a nap on her bed. He thought of how small his son had seemed in the center of the king-size mattress. And how defenseless he always looked when he slept. "Hell. It's obvious now," he said, planting one crutch as he pivoted to change direction. "He meant to hit Stefan, not me."

"Don't say that!" Marina stepped in front of David and grabbed his shoulders to halt his progress. "Don't even think it. Nothing's going to happen to that precious child. Nothing."

Her fingers pressed into a bruise, but David tuned out the discomfort. He was good at doing that. He'd had plenty of practice in shutting out pain; it was one of the earliest lessons he'd learned. "You're right," he said. "No one is going to hurt Stefan. I'll make sure of that."

"We both will. But what you're saying couldn't be true. Stefan trusts both of us. He would have told us if someone had mistreated him at either orphanage."

"He could have suppressed the memory just as he suppressed the memory of the accident that killed his parents."

She gave him a shake. "I can't believe that you're the one overreacting to this instead of me. David, calm down. You shouldn't keep pacing on crutches or you're going to wind up falling and hurting yourself worse."

"Marina—"

"Please," she said, gentling her grip. "We have to sort this out before Stefan wakes up."

As far as David was concerned, he'd already figured it out, only he'd almost been too late. The hit-and-run had been no accident. Stefan had valid reasons to be so afraid of the scarred man. God, this was worse than he'd suspected.

Marina moved her hands to his face. "David, think. As spooky as it seems, it could be just a strange coincidence. You can see that, can't you?"

He looked past her to the phone. "I don't have to wait for Gideon. I'll call each orphanage myself. You can translate for me. We'll describe this man to them and find out who he is."

"I went through the orphanage in Murmansk six times when I was searching for Stefan. I talked to every person who worked there or had any connection to the place, and I never saw anyone who resembled Stefan's monster."

"Then he has to be in St. Petersburg."

She flung her arms aside and stepped backward, muttering what sounded like a curse. "There are many other reasons Stefan could be having nightmares. Anyone can see that. Why are you so fixated on suspecting abuse in the first place? Is it because the orphanages are Russian?"

"That has nothing to do with it."

"Doesn't it? You're so determined to prove what a good parent you are, and how much better a life you can give Stefan in America than I can give him in Russia. You don't think Russians cherish their children as much as Americans do."

"You're way off base."

"Am I? Would you be as quick to assume abuse if the orphanage had been in America?"

David wedged his crutches in his armpits and reached for the buttons on his shirt.

"What are you doing?"

His fingers trembled as he shoved the buttons through the holes. "Showing you why you're wrong."

"By undressing?"

He shifted his weight to his good leg and shrugged the shirt off his left shoulder, shaking his arm free of the sleeve. "It's the only way you'll believe me."

Her forehead furrowed. "David…"

"Monsters can be anywhere, Marina," he said. He adjusted the crutch so he could peel his shirt over his bandaged arm. "They can be in Murmansk or Naples or Burlington, Vermont. Take a look at my back."

She didn't move. She was looking at his face instead of his body.

David dropped his shirt on the floor, braced the tip of one crutch solidly, and with the other turned himself to face away from her. "Children don't know how to tell people what's wrong, Marina. They try, but no one believes them."

Although she didn't make a sound, he could sense her shock. The hems of her pants whispered on the carpet as she drew nearer. She put her hand on his back, just as she had before, but this time there wasn't a barrier of cotton to dull the contact. She laid her palm between his shoulder blades, the only area that didn't bear any marks. "Oh, David," she murmured. "What happened?"

"I was placed in a foster home instead of an orphanage after my mother left me," he said. "The first one was fine, but it was overcrowded so I was transferred to another, and then another after that. My fourth foster home looked ideal. I was the only child with a middle-aged couple who ran a shoe store and went to church every Sunday. They didn't dress in black or have scars shaped like sickles. They weren't scary at all. Except when they drank."

She said something else in Russian. It didn't sound like a curse this time, though. She spread her fingers, her touch unsteady as she skimmed past the bruises he'd acquired yesterday to the marks he'd borne for almost thirty years.

David focused on his discarded shirt. He could feel her gaze move over his back as clearly as he felt her fingers. He knew what he looked like. The pockmarks and lines formed a macabre pattern. Most had flattened and distorted as he'd grown. A few of the thinner ones were barely visible, but the overall effect was as ugly as ugliness got.

"Are you saying your foster parents did this to you?" she asked, resting her fingertip on one of the dips.

"Only my foster father," he said. "He used his belt. It had a brass stud on the buckle that sometimes left a mark. It went on for almost a year. He called it discipline."

"How... My God, why didn't your foster mother stop him?"

"Shame. Embarrassment. Everyone believed they were nice people."

"This is from more than a belt." She traced her fingertip along one of the four ridges that angled downward across his rib cage. "I can see where there were stitches."

"The final night I spent there I knocked over the bastard's whiskey bottle when I stumbled after he hit me. It broke, so he picked up what was left of the neck and used it instead of his belt."

"Oh, my God!"

"That was the last time he touched me. My foster mother did such a bad job bandaging those slices I had to keep my coat on at school the next day so the blood on my shirt didn't show. My teacher noticed and took me to the hospital."

"Your teacher?"

"I had just started second grade. He listened to me, Marina. He was the first one who believed me. He made sure I never went back to those people." David shoved away the memories before they could swallow him and returned to the only topic that mattered. "You said I was fixated on suspecting abuse. You're right, I probably am. Even the remotest possibility of it pushes all my buttons."

"I can see why."

"Good. That was the point of this show-and-tell. And if I'm overreacting, that's good, too. I would give anything to be wrong about Stefan's monster, but I could never forgive myself if I was right and did nothing...."

His words trailed off. Not because he didn't know what to say. He still planned to check out the St. Petersburg orphanage whether Marina agreed to help him or not. He fell silent because he could feel her breath warm his back.

"I'm sorry, David," she whispered. "What you endured was unthinkable."

He clenched his jaw, conscious of how close her lips had to be to his skin. If he leaned back, or if she leaned forward, he would feel her mouth where he'd felt her fingers. It bothered him how much he wanted that.

She was an emotional woman, so naturally she had reacted to his story with compassion. She was open with her feelings and would be like this with anyone. He shouldn't take her response personally.

"I'm sorry I said that I wanted to smack you," she continued. "I didn't mean…"

"It's not the same thing, Marina. Not even remotely." He firmed his grip on his crutches and moved one step away from her. "I didn't show you my scars to get your sympathy," he said tightly.

"I realize that."

"So don't feel sorry for me."

"I'm not."

"I just wanted you to understand that I'm not condemning Russians or their child welfare system."

"I see that. I also understand why you were so tense all day. What you suspect happened with Stefan is bringing back your own nightmares."

"This isn't about me."

"How can you say that? Of course it's about you. It explains who you are. It's why you're so protective of Stefan, and why you believe in adoption so strongly. It's probably why you became a teacher."

Baring his body to her was one thing, but this was going further than he'd intended. He felt…exposed. "Marina, could you hand me my shirt?"

She made no move to pick it up. "Your teacher, the one who rescued you…"

"What about him?"

"His name was Anderson, wasn't it?"

"Yes."

Her breath hitched, as if she were fighting a sob. She moved past him and snatched his shirt from the floor. "Damn you, David."

"What?"

"You keep yourself buttoned up behind your starchiness and your boring clothes and try hard to make me dislike you but somehow you always wind up doing or saying something that makes me forget…" She shook her head.

"Makes you forget what?"

"Maybe it's not such a good idea if I understand you."

"Why not?"

She crumpled his shirt in her fists, turned to face him and lifted her chin. Her eyes brimmed with unshed tears. She'd cried countless times when she'd spoken about Stefan, but he knew these tears weren't for her nephew. She was looking at him the same way that she had yesterday at the medical center, just before she'd kissed him.

The hell with not taking her reaction personally. There probably wasn't a man alive who could resist that look. This time David didn't wait for her to make the first move. Balancing his weight on his good leg, he dropped one of his crutches, gripped the back of her head to hold her steady and brought his mouth to hers.

Marina melted into the kiss with a sigh. David anchored himself in the contact and silenced the warning that screamed through his head. He knew what he'd made her forget, because he wanted to forget it, too. At this moment, he wasn't kissing his enemy. He was kissing Marina.

He tilted his head to the angle they'd found the day before, the one that made the best fit, then pushed his fingers through her hair, losing himself in the scent of apples he stirred up. He didn't need the pressure of his hand to keep her where she was. She was stretching up to meet him, her lips trembling as she sealed her mouth to his.

She kissed as she did everything else, full out and un-inhibited. Now that she'd started, she didn't hesitate. She dropped his shirt and put both hands on his chest to steady herself, then lifted on her toes and parted her lips.

Desire kicked through his pulse at her wordless invita-tion. Yet he didn't plunge his tongue into her mouth all at once. He eased it slowly between her lips, giving her a chance to draw him in, sharing the intimacy instead of taking it, savoring her taste as honestly as she was enjoying his.

And she did enjoy him. David could feel it in the way she returned the kiss, and in the way she moved her fingers over his chest. She skimmed her palms across his mat of hair, fol-lowing the contours of his muscles, touching him with a boldness she hadn't used on his back. He leaned forward until he could feel her breasts nudge his chest. Through the gauzy fabric of her tunic he could feel her nipples tighten in response. Instinctively he stepped closer…

The next thing he knew, he was falling sideways. He jammed the crutch he still held into his armpit and made a series of small hops before he slapped his free hand against the wall to regain his balance.

Marina blinked, then picked up the crutch that he'd dropped on the floor earlier and held it out to him. Her hand shook. "Are you all right?"

Blood pounded in his knee and each one of his bruises. He breathed deeply a few times, trying to clear his head. The pain was returning him to his senses more effectively than a cold shower could have. "Yeah." He took the crutch from her and fitted it under his arm. "I'm fine."

She licked her upper lip, her tongue tracing the moisture he had left there. "I, uh, forgot your condition."

That's not all we forgot. "So did I."

She looked at his bandaged knee. "You should sit down."

"I should leave."

"Stefan's still sleeping."

"He's napped long enough."

"You told Gideon to call here."

"I'll talk to him later."

"But—"

"Do you still want me to answer that question?"

"What question?"

"When we were out by the pool, you wanted to know why I kissed you."

She raked her hair over her shoulder, then tugged on the hem of her tunic. "You did it because you felt like it," she said. "It's the same reason I kissed you this time. Sometimes it's easier to express feelings physically than with words. It's a natural outcome of strong emotion. Exceptional circumstances. A momentary impulse."

"It's more than momentary, Marina. I've been wanting to kiss you for the past five days."

She glanced at his chest. "Really, it's probably better if we don't analyze this."

"You claimed you preferred being honest."

"Of course I do."

"Then you should know that every time you smile at me

or touch me, I've been tempted to kiss you. Even when you argue with me, I find myself looking at your mouth and thinking of more pleasant ways you could use it."

"David—"

"Just the way you say my name with that accent of yours sounds like a caress."

"Then why do you sound so angry about it?"

"Why? *Why?* Because you're the last woman on earth I should want to kiss. You want to take away my son!"

She picked up his shirt again and slapped it against her leg. "He's not *your* son, he's *my* nephew."

"There! You see? We can't forget, even for a minute. Kissing you again would be the dumbest thing that I could do." He planted the tips of his crutches in front of her feet and leaned over her. "But now that I know what your mouth feels like, it's going to be hell not to come back for more."

A familiar gleam of challenge sparked in her eyes. "It's not as if I'm asking you to."

"I know you're not. This isn't what we want from each other."

"Exactly. It's not why we're here. We had this conversation already, David."

"So are we agreed it won't happen again, Marina?"

"Agreed."

"Perfect. Then stop looking at me as if you cared."

"Fine. Then don't tell me any more stories that make me like you. And from now on—" She shoved the shirt at his chest and turned away. "Keep your clothes on."

CHAPTER NINE

THE LIQUID SOUND of harp music flowed through the Rose Petal tearoom as gently as morning mist. Ivy trailed from pottery urns, glossy and lush against the walnut wainscoting. Crisp chintz in subdued pastel hues covered the chairs and old-fashioned settees. The same understated colors gleamed from the porcelain teacups and teapots that rested on dark, delicately carved wood tables. From its place of honor on the wall, a portrait of Alexandra Rhys-Williams Stamos, the late wife of the ship's owner, presided graciously over the guests. It was in memory of Alexandra that every detail in the room was designed to evoke an English country garden.

As lovely as the room was, though, Marina had thought it was a ridiculous place to bring an active five-year-old. Olena had repeatedly warned her to keep Stefan away from breakables, and even Marina could see that a single nudge against one of those elegant tables could send half a dozen cups and saucers crashing to the floor. Passengers came to this tearoom for peace and civilized conversation. It wouldn't be fair to expect a child to sit still for the length of time it would take to empty even the smallest teapot.

Yet David had had an entirely different purpose in mind when he'd added the Rose Petal to his schedule. He'd bypassed the tables and had gone straight to the curving gold harp that sat in the center of the room. He'd used the tip of his crutch to slide a footstool next to the harpist and had asked the woman if Stefan could sit there while she played.

Word of David's accident had spread through the ship's personnel days ago, and everyone from the cruise director to the hotel manager was doing their best to make the remainder of his voyage pleasant. So naturally, the harpist had complied with his request. More than that, she'd insisted on dragging a chair next to Stefan's stool herself so David could join his son while he listened to the music.

What woman could have resisted a request from David? Although the scrapes on his cheek and forehead were healing, and he was regaining his mobility at an impressive rate, he still carried the ruggedly vulnerable, appealing air of a wounded warrior. Even without knowing the story behind his current injuries, anyone would be sympathetic. Any normal person would feel a tug on their heartstrings. It was perfectly natural. Nothing to worry about. It didn't mean anything other than her emotions were functioning properly.

Marina sighed. Almost three full days had gone by since the accident in Naples. Perhaps in another three she could convince herself her feelings for David were nothing to worry about.

The harpist finished the sedate Bach prelude she'd been playing, winked at Stefan and launched into a more spirited selection by Rimsky-Korsakov. Stefan leaned his shoulder against David's good knee and bobbed his head to the music. David looked past the frame of the harp to meet Marina's gaze and arched one eyebrow smugly.

Great. He'd not only contrived the perfect activity for

Stefan, he'd managed to bring a little piece of Russia into an English tearoom. She brought her hands together silently to mime applause, then picked up her teacup and pretended to be engrossed in the floral arrangement next to her table.

David had thrown himself back into their custody debate with a vengeance, taking every opportunity to demonstrate what a good parent he would be. He hadn't given her any more peeks into his past; he hadn't kissed her again, either. Or taken off any clothing. As a matter of fact, he was going out of his way not to touch her. He seemed to be doing just what she'd asked, trying his best to make her not like him.

But it was too late for that. He still aggravated her regularly, yet she liked the ingenuity he showed in their ongoing debate. She was even starting to like that smug little twinkle he got in his eyes when he scored a point.

But that's all it was. She liked him. Nothing else. Oh, and she found him increasingly attractive—there was that whole wounded warrior appeal. And although it might be twisted to enjoy watching the muscles of his arms and shoulders flex as he used his crutches, it was impossible for any female not to appreciate what superb condition he was in. Marina wasn't bothered by his dull clothes anymore, either. She suspected he'd acquired the habit of trying to make himself appear as unnoticeable as possible when he'd been a child at the mercy of those monsters masquerading as foster parents....

Her teacup clattered as she returned it to its saucer. At times she wished he hadn't shown her those marks on his back. She could no longer look at him the same. She'd already begun to admire him for the man he was, but now that she knew what he'd gone through to become that man, her respect for him had only deepened.

Considering what David had endured, it was a wonder he could be remotely rational about the creature from Stefan's nightmares. To say the situation pushed his buttons was an understatement. Because of Ariana's eyewitness account of the accident, Gideon had finally agreed to relay David's concerns about the orphanages in St. Petersburg and Murmansk to the Russian police, and he'd been very tolerant of David's demands to keep looking in spite of the fact no tall, scarred man had been reported at either institution. Yet that was as far as the security chief's cooperation had extended.

Gideon shared Marina's opinion that the similarity between the hit-and-run driver in Naples and Stefan's description of his monster was likely coincidence. According to the Naples police, the actual owner of the taxi had been found murdered, so whoever had been driving the vehicle had probably been speeding because he'd been fleeing the crime scene. The Italian authorities were concentrating their investigation on the taxi owner's enemies. They'd found nothing to support David's theory that Stefan had been deliberately targeted.

Still, David hadn't allowed Stefan to go ashore since then. The ship was currently docked at Alghero, on the island of Sardinia, yet David had chosen to spend the morning in the Rose Petal instead of going on a tour. He claimed his knee would make an excursion too uncomfortable, and while there was some truth in that, his primary concern was Stefan's safety.

Marina realized she was missing a golden opportunity, but she hadn't yet breathed a word of David's paranoia to Rudolph. She should, though. She didn't owe David any loyalty—he was trying to take away her nephew. She needed to capitalize on every chance she could get to discredit his suitability as a parent.

Yet she couldn't find it in her heart to use David's anxieties in order to score points against him. He'd bared his scars and his past to her because he'd wanted her to understand his worries about Stefan, regardless of the harm it might do to his custody case. His intentions had been good.

Besides, the days confined to the ship hadn't done Stefan any harm. He hadn't had another nightmare, and although he'd imagined seeing his monster a few times when they passed near a man who was tall or was dressed in black, he'd been readily comforted by a hug and a few soft words. She suspected that could be why he "saw" it, because he felt the need for comfort and knew that was one sure way to get it. Once he came home with her and he was back in his native land, he probably would forget all about the monster.

The Rimsky-Korsakov melody ended in a flourish of showy arpeggios. The echoes of the final notes were sweetened with the sound of Stefan's delighted laughter.

Marina returned her attention to the center of the room. Her nephew had risen from the footstool and was standing beside the harp. The harpist stroked her fingertips over the strings and motioned to Stefan to do the same. The huge instrument was almost twice as tall as he was and nothing like the balalaika he'd seen his father play. Still, it had strings, too, so he didn't hesitate to try.

Leaving her tea unfinished, Marina went to join them. "That's pretty, Stevochki," she said.

He grinned and ran his fingers across the shortest strings near the instrument's neck. "Bird," he said.

"Hey, that does sound like a bird," David said.

The harpist took Stefan's hand in hers and guided their fingers to pluck a series of notes. Stefan responded enthusiastically, humming the melody as they played it.

Marina glanced at David. He was smiling as he watched her nephew, not a warrior now, but a doting parent. He was going to miss Stefan terribly when the adoption was reversed.

Crossing her arms, Marina tried to ignore the regret that followed that thought. This was why it would be better if she didn't like him. Only one of them could win. She didn't want to hurt him, but that's what would happen when she gained custody of Stefan. David would get over it, though. He'd known Stefan for only a week. It took much longer than that to develop a real emotional attachment, didn't it?

The same applied to any relationship, including one between two adults. A woman could like a man, and admire him and sympathize with him, too. And a physical attraction didn't take long to develop. Sometimes the source of passion could be confused, though, such as when two antagonists mistook the adrenaline from a quarrel for something else. But love was rare and special. No one could actually start to love someone after merely a week, right?

God, she hoped that was true.

Marina finally recognized the tune Stefan and the harpist were picking out. It was the theme from *Doctor Zhivago*.

A timely reminder of all the unhappy endings in Russian love stories.

THE TAVERNA MIKE HAD found was miles from the harbor. It was small, dim and staffed with the kind of people who would sooner roll a tourist than serve one. The chances of someone from *Alexandra's Dream* noticing him here were slim, and even if someone did see him, the odds of anyone recognizing him were next to nil. When he was in costume, people only saw Father Connelly's collar. Without it, he was just another man sipping whiskey.

So he took his time as he leaned his elbow on the bar, brought the glass to his lips and savored the final mouthful. The room wavered a little more than he'd expected as he made his way to the door. He didn't mind—he hoped there was still some of the buzz left when he got back to the ship since it would make it easier for him to look amiable. He had yet to make his pickup. He'd been to Alghero before, though, and knew the address wasn't far.

He located the antique shop after only a few wrong turns. The street was too narrow and at the wrong angle for sunlight to penetrate past the upper stories of the buildings, making the place almost as dim as the bar had been. That, plus the whiskey buzz, was why he was slow to recognize the woman who was studying the display of porcelain near the back wall.

"Father Connelly?" she asked.

He started, his gaze whipping to the tall brunette who had spoken. Of all the stores in Alghero, what the hell was she doing in this one? "Why, Miss Bennett," he said, automatically slipping into character. "What a pleasant surprise."

She gestured vaguely around the room. "I was exploring today and found this place by accident. They have some lovely pieces here. I'm not sure if I can afford them, but I love to look, don't you?"

Mike waited for his eyes to adjust so he could see her face more clearly. She sounded awkward, maybe even a little nervous. "Ah, you know I have a weakness for a good funeral urn."

The librarian began chattering again, definitely appearing uneasy. Mike realized he hadn't put his collar back on. Could that be the source of her discomfort? He commented on the warm afternoon, hoping she'd conclude he'd doffed the collar due to the temperature.

Regardless, he couldn't risk making the pickup now. He caught the eye of the man who entered the shop from the back room and shook his head, silently conveying the message not to approach. Their boss wouldn't like this, but Mike could always double up the next time the ship stopped at Sardinia.

Hiding his frustration beneath one of Father Connelly's benign smiles, Mike left Ariana in the antique shop and headed for the harbor. A shuttle bus was unloading a group of people at the pier. Mike ducked behind the corner of a building to put his collar back on before anyone else saw him. He had just finished tucking it into place when he noticed that he wasn't alone.

A tall man stood in an arched doorway less than a yard away. He was dressed all in black, which should have made his pale face hard to miss, yet he seemed to know exactly how to blend into the shadows. He held himself completely motionless, like a hunter stalking his prey....

The last of the whiskey buzz cleared from Mike's head in a flash. Could the man be a cop? Had someone tipped the authorities about the smuggling scheme?

He tamped down the reflexive urge to run, forcing himself to remain in character. The boss was supposed to have high-placed connections at Interpol and would have let him know if anyone was sniffing around their operation. And no local cop would bother doing a fishing expedition on *Alexandra's Dream*—the Stamos family name made the ship above suspicion.

The man flicked his gaze across Mike, then returned his attention to the shuttle bus on the pier, apparently dismissing a priest as beneath his interest.

Despite the warmth of the day, Mike felt the hair rise on the back of his neck. That was no cop, he decided as he headed for the ship. Those black eyes had been as dead as a shark's. And no one got a scar as nasty-looking as that guy's by playing on the right side of the law.

They'd already had enough trouble on this trip, with a crewman being murdered in Croatia and a passenger being hit by a car in Naples. Mike didn't want the cops to have another reason to visit the ship. He didn't need any increased scrutiny. Keeping the genuine goods in his stateroom with his collection of fakes might not be such a smart idea—it would be tough to claim innocence if a cop found them there.

Mike hoped whatever the scarred man was up to, he'd have the sense to keep his business on shore.

DAVID PULLED STEFAN'S PLATE toward him and cut the chicken into bite-size morsels. He was aware that he was using far more force than necessary and was running the risk of driving the French silverplate right through the Limoges china, but venting his frustration on a piece of chicken was better than reaching across the table and…

And what? He wasn't sure what he'd do if he finally allowed himself to touch Marina. That's why he'd been avoiding it. It was also why he was reacting so strongly to her offer—it was getting more and more difficult to keep his emotions under control with her. "Buttoned up," she'd said. Fine. That's how he lived, and it had always worked for him.

"It really wouldn't be any trouble," she went on. "I can

see that Stefan enjoys your company, and it would be good for him to have the opportunity to practice his English. I plan to keep it up, by the way."

David finished shredding the chicken and started on the snow peas that were fanned artistically on the edge of the plate.

"My apartment is enormous. You're welcome to visit."

"How very generous of you."

"Or if you prefer not to fly all the way to Moscow, we could meet when Stefan and I travel to some other city. What about Paris or London?"

He concentrated on laying the knife as quietly as possible on his own plate, then slid the mangled dinner in front of his son. *His* son, he reminded himself. In spite of the ongoing pressure from Marina's lawyer, Harold had assured David that his adoption was still valid. Besides, it was only a matter of days before Stefan would be safely on American soil.

But for how long? David had made no progress in his campaign to change Marina's mind. Quite the contrary. She'd become more intractable than ever. And now she had the cheek to offer him visiting privileges, as if her custody of Stefan was a foregone conclusion.

She picked up a linen napkin that had been folded into the shape of a stork, flapped it at her nephew a few times to make him smile, then shook it out and tucked it beneath his chin. Leaning her head toward his, she spoke to him in Russian for a while, evidently talking about the dining room, judging by the gestures she made toward the decor.

David moved her wineglass out of range of her hand. If there were to be any disasters at the table, they would probably be due to Marina, not Stefan.

This was their first visit to the Empire Room, the ship's main dining room. Until now, David had gone for the more casual dining options so that he didn't keep Stefan up too late, but he'd decided they might as well try dressing up and dining in style one night. It would be a good experience for Stefan. It had nothing to do with the fact that Marina was getting restless from remaining on board for more than three days straight and would enjoy doing something different.

No, why should he care about entertaining her? And how could he keep noticing how beautiful she was when they were the midst of a disagreement?

He didn't really need to ask himself those questions. He knew this dinner was for Marina's sake as much as for Stefan's. As for noticing Marina's appearance, that was nothing new. David had realized from the start that she wasn't the kind of woman that anyone could ignore.

She was more appetizing than the meal, as the rest of the men in the room must have noticed. Although her dress covered her from her neck to her wrists, the fabric glimmered with her slightest movement, showing off her curves rather than hiding them. It was the color of cream, which was an unusual departure from Marina's typically exuberant hues, so it made the green of her eyes appear more vivid, and made her hair gleam like spun platinum. She'd tried to pile her hair on top of her head, but it had been escaping its gold clip all evening to tumble around her face and down her nape. One lock in particular kept swinging against the corner of her jaw, drawing his gaze to her mouth....

"If the cost of the trip presents a problem," she said, "I could arrange your airfare."

David picked up his knife and got to work on his own meal. "I don't need anyone's charity."

"I meant no offense. I'm trying to be practical, since I do have more money than you."

"Yes, you've pointed that out on several occasions."

She lifted one eyebrow. "You're not one of those men who get self-conscious about the, ah, size of his wallet, are you, David?"

Damn, he shouldn't enjoy sparring with her so much. "The size of my wallet has never posed a problem, Marina. I am exceptionally skilled at making the most of my resources."

"How enterprising."

"But even though I enjoy boasting about my skills as much as any man, I'm not letting you change the subject."

She pursed her lips.

"The fact remains," he continued, "you're not in a position to offer me visitation."

"You offered me the same thing. No," she said, holding up her palm. "I'm wrong. It wasn't the same thing. You didn't mention anything about where I would stay, so my offer is more generous than yours."

Stefan looked from David to Marina, his fork stalled between his plate and his mouth. A piece of chicken wobbled on the end of the fork tines.

Marina shifted her hand and cupped her palm under Stefan's fork, catching the chicken just as it fell. She held it between her fingers and zoomed it around a few times, making a burring sound with her lips like an airplane, then popped it into Stefan's mouth and smiled. "It's something for you to consider, David," she said. "It wasn't an insult."

Her smile was for Stefan, not him, he reminded himself. They were getting plenty of practice smiling at each other and using a pleasant tone, no matter what they were saying. At the rate Stefan was picking up English, though, they wouldn't have the privacy of the language barrier for long.

Then again, by the time Stefan did understand enough English to follow their conversation, there wouldn't be any more conversations like this. Everything would be said through their lawyers in a courtroom.

Stefan stabbed another piece of chicken and waved his fork, imitating the airplane noise that Marina had made. The food flew off the end of the fork on the third pass and plopped into David's water glass. Stefan's smile disappeared.

"Thank you, son," David said calmly, dipping his little finger into his glass. He dabbed his fingertip against his tongue as if testing the taste, then nodded. "Chicken soup's one of my favorites."

Marina pressed her lips together, her eyes sparkling with laughter, then hitched her chair closer to Stefan's and translated David's comment into Russian.

The uncertainty cleared from Stefan's face. "Soup," he said, his smile returning. "Chicken soup! I like soup!"

David was pleased that Stefan had added another few words to his vocabulary, regardless of how it had happened. He'd worry about the lesson in table manners some other time. "That's right," he said. "I like chicken soup."

Stefan pointed at the vegetables on his plate and made an expression that David needed no help translating.

"I don't like snow peas," David said.

"I don't like snow peas," Stefan repeated immediately. He pointed to other items on the table, obviously enjoying the ability to express himself, then settled down to eat the foods that he liked. Mercifully, the rest of the meal progressed without any more airplane sound effects.

David could understand how Marina's sister must have gotten exasperated with her behavior at times. Marina was overindulgent and didn't always set the best example. She was also a stranger to the concepts of schedules and nutrition. He firmly believed he would do a better job as a parent. Still, her devotion to her nephew was beyond doubt, as was his affection for his aunt. Stefan was going to miss her when they went home.

And he wasn't the only one.

That was the main reason her invitation to visit her in Moscow had nettled him. Not because she was presuming she would win her case. Her offer had brought home the fact that within a matter of days, they would be living on opposite sides of the world.

He didn't want to admit to himself that he would miss her. He'd known from the start it was pointless to feel anything for her. The only thing she wanted from him was his child.

He'd been wrong when he'd told her that she wasn't anything like Ellie. The two women didn't look alike, or share the same character traits, yet they did have something in common. All his wife had wanted from him at the end was a child. Ellie had stayed with him, slept with him, pretended to love him, only because she'd wanted a baby.

The food David was eating suddenly tasted like dust. He swallowed and reached for his water, then looked blankly at the morsel of chicken that was in the bottom of his glass. He shouldn't compare Marina and Ellie. His ex-wife wouldn't have been caught dead playing airplane with a child's food in a place like this. Not only were they completely different women, the situation was different, too.

Marina had always been honest about her priorities. She wasn't pretending anything.

And he had no illusions about Marina. True, she was an interesting woman. Her wit and her quicksilver moods were as stimulating as her appearance. Yet there was a vast difference between enjoying someone's company and having serious feelings for them. An emotion like love didn't happen overnight. Love was a long-term commitment, not an impulse. He'd known Ellie for ten years before they'd married. He'd considered everything carefully and she'd seemed like the perfect match for him.

Even so, he'd been wrong.

"If it bothers you that much," Marina said, "you should have the waiter bring you a fresh one."

David realized he was still looking at his glass. He glanced around the dining room. A few of the serving staff were gliding between the tables, bringing drinks or topping up water glasses, but David didn't try to signal anyone. He couldn't care less about a bit of food in his water.

Stefan's fork clanked to his plate. Without a word, he twisted on his chair and slid backward under the white tablecloth.

Marina scowled at David. "You were staring at your water for so long, he thinks you're angry about the chicken."

David sighed and put down his glass. "Stefan," he said. "It's okay. I like chicken soup."

Stefan remained silent. He bumped into David's good knee, then wrapped his arm around David's calf.

Marina leaned to the side and lifted up an edge of the tablecloth. "Stevovoichski?"

Stefan pressed into David's foot and snatched the tablecloth down so quickly the glasses wobbled.

"You shouldn't have brought him here," Marina said. "It's too formal for a child."

"There wouldn't have been a problem if you hadn't encouraged him to play with his food."

"One wayward fragment is not a serious offense."

"You'd think differently if you were the one who had to clean up."

"As long as he's eating, I would dress him in a raincoat and let him have his dinner in my bathtub."

She probably would, David thought, his lips twitching as he pictured the scene. "Hey, buddy," he said, reaching beneath the table. He found Stefan's shoulder and gave him a reassuring pat. "Come back. Everything's fine."

Stefan's shoulder was shaking. He grabbed David's hand tightly between both of his. "Monster," he whispered.

David's humor vanished. He squeezed Stefan's fingers gently. "It's all right, son. You're safe with me. I promise, there are no more monsters now."

"Monster!" Stefan repeated, then launched into a string of Russian words.

"He says the monster's here," Marina translated. "In the dining room."

David tightened his grasp on Stefan and stretched up in his chair to scan the room. The staff were all wearing white jackets, but many of the male passengers were wearing dark suits. One of the men must have reminded Stefan of his monster. That was the only explanation. Unless...

Oh, hell! Had the scarred man managed to get on board? Was he here? The ship was supposed to be secure. Gideon had been emphatic about that. There were a series of identity checks for anyone boarding, as well as regular patrols and video surveillance of all the public areas. There were also more confidential measures that the security chief hadn't wanted to go into detail about. That's why David had felt comfortable keeping Stefan on board. It was the safest place to stay while the police continued to check out the orphanages. Yet what if—

"David, no." Marina reached across the table and grasped his arm. "I can see what you're thinking, but he's not here."

David focused on a tuxedoed man who was getting up from a table near the service doors. He was turned away, though, so David couldn't tell if he had a scar. Another tall man with a black jacket was standing near the dining room entrance, but he had a beard.

Marina rose from her chair so she could shift her hand to David's cheek. "There's no monster," she said. "It's okay."

He snapped his gaze to hers. She'd used the same tone with him that he'd used with Stefan, but she wasn't mocking him. Her eyes shone with sympathy, just as they had when he'd shown her his back.

He never should have done that. He didn't want her pity, and he sure as hell didn't want her touch to feel so good.

But all the cautions in his head couldn't stop the warmth that raced through his senses. It was only her palm against his cheek, not her lips, or her tongue, yet the connection was even stronger than the last time. He had a crazy urge to reach out and pull her into his arms, tell her more, show her more…

This was why he couldn't think about her leaving. He didn't want this to end. She'd seen the ugliness and hadn't run. Instead, she'd looked past it.

What the hell was the matter with him? All he wanted from her was Stefan. They had this much straight.

He drew back his head, breaking the contact with her hand. "Stefan's tired. We'll skip dessert."

Instead of backing off, she braced her fingertips beside his plate and brought her face close to his. "I understand why you're doing this," she said, her voice low and urgent. "And I realize I know nothing about raising children, so don't bother reminding me how inept I am, but even I can see there's a very simple reason why Stefan is underneath the table."

"What?"

"He's trying to get your attention," she said.

David wanted to deny it. He owed it to Stefan to believe him, didn't he? Just as David's father had believed him when no one else would…

That sounded irrational, even to him. He'd already acknowledged that he couldn't be objective about this. There still was no evidence to support his worries about Stefan. Marina might be right. His own reaction might be reinforcing Stefan's behavior.

He took another look around the dining room, this time finally noticing the heads that were turned toward them. He rubbed his face, giving himself a few seconds to regain control, then pushed aside Stefan's empty chair and flipped up the tablecloth.

Stefan was sitting on the floor with his knees pulled to his chest. He was sucking his thumb, his eyes wide as he looked at David.

"Let's go, Stefan," David said. "Trust me, there's no monster here."

Stefan shook his head and curled his arm more tightly around David's calf.

Marina hitched up her skirt and squatted to bring her face down to Stefan's level. She spoke briefly in Russian, then held out her hand.

Keeping his thumb in his mouth, Stefan released David's leg and inched out from beneath the table. He peeked over the edge toward the dining room entrance.

"What did you tell him?" David asked.

She straightened and took Stefan's hand. "I told him you threw water on the monster and it dissolved. That often works in fairy tales."

Leave it to Marina to get to the heart of the matter, David thought. Stefan didn't want to be told the monster was gone, he wanted to hear that it was dead.

Damn, he was going to miss her. They both would. David gathered his crutches and got to his feet. "Thank you."

"I also promised to give him dessert," she said, starting off with Stefan in tow. "I'll order a cheesecake from room service."

He followed them between the tables. "I'll take care of him, Marina. I don't want him getting overtired."

She glanced at him over her shoulder as she walked. "Don't worry, we'll leave some for you."

"Marina—"

"Don't be a grouch," she said.

"I'm not a grouch. I'm being a responsible parent."

She flicked her fingers at him and headed for the exit.

David stared at her back. He was no longer finding that finger-flick of hers irritating. He was getting used to it, just like her lightning mood changes. He increased his pace as much as his crutches allowed. He reached the doorway just as a pair of men stepped through.

One was Gideon Dayan. "Mr. Anderson," he said, moving in front of David. "We need to speak with you."

David glanced at Gideon's companion. He was a middle-aged man of average height, with a weathered face and the stance of a bulldog. Although he wore a tweed sport coat instead of an officer's white uniform like the security chief, he had the look of someone in law enforcement.

Gideon confirmed David's guess with his next words. "This is Captain Enzo Locatelli from the international crime unit of the Italian State Police," he said. "He has news that concerns your son."

CHAPTER TEN

THE PHOTOGRAPH WAS grainy, obviously taken from a distance and enlarged, yet there were enough details to make the man recognizable. His steel-gray hair was cut military-short, leaving nothing to soften the prominent bone structure of his face. He had a high forehead and prominent brows over dark eyes set deeply in their sockets. His nose was broad and flat like the blade of a shovel. His mouth was only a tight slash in his pale face, but that seemed more because of his expression than the shape of his lips. All this would have made his face memorable, yet his most distinctive feature was the thick, white line that arced across his left cheek from the outer edge of the cheekbone to the side of his chin.

Marina crossed her arms tightly across her chest, feeling a chill that had nothing to do with the air-conditioning in her stateroom.

Good God, that man was real.

"His name is Ilya Fedorovich," Captain Locatelli said, laying the photograph on the dining table. "This is the most recent picture Interpol had. The Russian police took it two years ago during their surveillance of a heroin-smuggling operation in Vladivostok that was run by the Russian mob."

David propped one crutch against the table and reached

out to slide the photo in front of him. "And you claim he's a hit man?"

"He's a ruthless assassin who works for whoever will pay his fee. Interpol provided our office with an extensive file on this individual. Fedorovich once was a colonel in the Soviet Red Army, a decorated hero of their war with Afghanistan, but after the breakup of the Soviet Union he turned to private practice."

Interpol. The Russian *Mafiya*. A hit man. Even with that scarred face staring out from the photograph, this was hard to believe. Rubbing her palms over her sleeves, Marina looked at the three men who stood around the table. Like David, neither Gideon nor Locatelli had elected to sit. The discussion was too serious for them to consider their comfort.

Yet David had considered Stefan's comfort, she thought, her gaze straying toward the bedroom. They were holding this meeting in her stateroom rather than the security center because David hadn't wanted to leave Stefan, nor had he wanted to alarm him. Stefan was safely tucked into her bed, a CD of children's music playing softly on the bedroom sound system. It had taken a while to get him to sleep, though. He kept wanting them to reassure him that David had really gotten rid of his monster.

She glanced back at David. He was still wearing the charcoal-gray suit that he'd donned for dinner, but he'd loosened his tie and opened the top few buttons of his shirt. It was hard to believe that less than an hour ago she'd been enjoying his company and thinking about how handsome he had looked tonight. And she'd been moved by how earnestly he'd reacted to what she'd thought was nothing….

Oh, God, this had to be a nightmare.

Marina moved beside him, her attention drawn back to

the photo of the hit man. "This must be a mistake," she said. "Another coincidence. Stefan couldn't have had anything to do with a man like this."

"What's his connection to the orphanages that Stefan was in?" David asked.

"He has none," Locatelli replied. "But the Russian police believe Fedorovich was in Murmansk last summer. They've found evidence that the same organization that had been smuggling Afghanistan heroin out of Vladivostok has been setting up a new pipeline for it in Murmansk."

"And this Fedorovich was working for the drug smugglers?" Marina asked.

"That's why it took so long for the Russian authorities to get back to me," Gideon said. "They were concentrating on checking the Murmansk and St. Petersburg orphanages for possible child abusers."

"It was fortunate that someone from their organized crime division recognized the description the boy gave and tipped off Interpol," Locatelli said. "Apparently they've been amassing data on Fedorovich for years. He's wanted by several law enforcement agencies but no one has been able to apprehend him."

"I still don't see how this could involve Stefan," Marina said. "He's just a child."

"His father was a fisherman."

"Yes, he was."

"I understand that most of the fishing boats in Murmansk sell their catches to foreign factory ships," Locatelli said. "From there, crates of fish are distributed throughout the world. It's an excellent method for smuggling contraband."

"Borya would never have dealt with smugglers. He was

too proud—" Marina caught her breath, grabbing on to the table to steady herself. "That's it! Borya."

David wrapped his free arm around her shoulders and drew her to his side. She leaned against him, grateful for the contact. She didn't want to finish her thought, but the pieces moved into place anyway.

The mob would need a way to transport their drugs. Borya owned a fishing boat. But stubborn, honest Borya wouldn't have agreed to smuggle anything. A hit man had been in Murmansk last summer....

"Last August. The accident." She stopped, unable to get the rest of the words out.

David squeezed her shoulder. "Stefan's parents were killed in a car accident," he said to the policeman. "Is it possible that Fedorovich was responsible for it?"

Locatelli looked at each of them in turn. "Yes. The Russian authorities believe the mob hired Fedorovich to eliminate the entire Gorsky family. They're still investigating whether Borya had been involved with the mob and had been caught trying to cheat them."

"No," Marina said. "That's impossible. My brother-in-law was an honest man."

"If he was, then the mob could have wanted him killed in order to intimidate other fishermen into cooperating," Locatelli continued. "Either way, the death of his family would have been meant to serve as an example."

"My sister and brother-in-law were murdered," Marina said. "Oh, God. Stefan was in the car with them. He must have seen…"

"Stefan saw Fedorovich," David said. "*This* is what he's been trying to tell us. It had nothing to do with the orphanage. I was completely wrong."

"Regardless of why you set the investigation into motion, Mr. Anderson," Gideon said, "it's a good thing that you did. Otherwise, no one would have made the connections."

"Mr. Dayan is correct," Locatelli said. "Once the Russian police realized Fedorovich was involved and they contacted Interpol, the clues came together quickly. The bullet that killed a Russian crewman from *Alexandra's Dream* in Dubrovnik was fired from the same 9 mm Makarov as the bullet that killed the owner of the taxi that struck Mr. Anderson in Naples. Interpol matched both to one of Fedorovich's confirmed victims."

"It appears the hit man has been following *Alexandra's Dream*," Gideon said.

Marina shivered. This was essentially what David had suspected, only she had thought he was being paranoid. She slid her arms around his waist, struggling to process the information. "Why?"

"He's after Stefan," David said.

Locatelli nodded. "The boy is in grave danger. Fedorovich must have discovered he escaped the crash that killed his parents."

"But Stefan's only a child," Marina exclaimed. "He's no threat. Even if his memory of the accident comes back, he's too young for his testimony to be taken seriously."

"That isn't the reason Fedorovich is tracking him," Locatelli said. "According to his file, the man has made his reputation on his perfect record. He hasn't failed to complete a contract yet. He's obsessed with killing. He views it as his duty and pursues it as relentlessly as a military campaign. It's one of the reasons he's been impossible to catch. Until now, his target became known only after the fact."

David tensed. "You didn't come here only to warn us. You came here to use Stefan as bait."

Marina was still reeling from the revelations up to now, but this one brought her mind back into focus. She could see the truth of David's accusation in the faces of the men on the other side of the table. "Bait," she repeated. "You can't possibly plan to dangle my nephew in front of this killer."

"Fedorovich doesn't know that law enforcement is a step ahead of him," Locatelli said. "That's why I flew to Sardinia and boarded this ship tonight before it left Alghero. This could be the only opportunity to draw him out. We need to act swiftly to take advantage of it."

David withdrew his arm from Marina's shoulders and used one crutch to hobble around the table. He stopped when he stood toe-to-toe with the policeman. "Get this straight. Under no circumstances will I permit anyone to jeopardize my son's safety."

Locatelli stood his ground, in spite of the fact David was a head taller than him. "Fedorovich obviously knows the itinerary of *Alexandra's Dream,* so he's sure to be waiting in Palermo when we arrive there tomorrow morning."

"Then there's no way in hell I'm taking Stefan off the ship."

"You misunderstood me. We want you to stay here where we can control the situation. At this point, you don't need to go ashore, just book a tour or arrange transportation as if you were. Our men will be watching the port. The instant Fedorovich shows his face, we'll arrest him."

"What will you do if he slips past you?" David demanded. "If he gets on this ship, Stefan's a sitting duck."

"Our people will be working with Mr. Dayan's staff to

ensure that doesn't happen. I've already briefed Captain Pappas on our strategy and he has agreed to cooperate. With the security systems that are already in place, and the extra measures we'll be adding when we reach port tomorrow, there will be little risk to other passengers, yet if we remove you from the ship, we would have to do so under guard and that would be sure to alert Fedorovich. The captain understands that if we don't capitalize on this opportunity to apprehend Fedorovich now, Stefan will be in more serious peril. This could be our only chance to arrest a killer and to save your son's life."

Marina snatched the photograph from the table and shook it at Locatelli. "You don't expect us to simply sit here and wait for this murderer to turn up, do you? You must be out of your mind."

"The boy will be safest in this controlled environment until Fedorovich is caught," he persisted. "It really is the only option."

"No, it isn't." She dropped the photo and looked at David. "You can take Stefan to America."

"Miss Artamova," Locatelli began.

"Get Stefan off the ship tonight," she continued. "Before we reach Palermo. I'll charter a helicopter to meet the ship while we're still at sea, so Fedorovich won't know you took Stefan away."

David stared at her. "You would do that?"

"I would do anything."

"That won't work," Locatelli said. "Fedorovich is sure to hear of it."

"It will keep Stefan safe." She waved her arm toward the telephone. "My lawyer can arrange the plane tickets. He's good at that sort of thing. By the time Fedorovich realizes Stefan is no longer here, David will have my nephew on the other side of the world."

Even as she spoke the words, she felt a wound open in her heart. A week ago, she couldn't have imagined saying this. It was the very thing she'd vowed to prevent.

But the issue of custody was the last thing she cared about. Stefan's life was at stake. The mere thought of anyone hurting the child she loved made everything else irrelevant. "My nephew will be safe in America with you," she said, returning her gaze to David. "I can trust you to protect him. He'll be far away from this Russian madman."

"I'm afraid that's not true, Miss Artamova," Locatelli said. "Ilya Fedorovich has been active in more than a dozen countries, which is what brought him to Interpol's attention in the first place. According to their information, borders are no obstacle to him. He speaks several languages, including English. Taking the boy to America might delay Fedorovich, but it won't deter him. This man will not give up. Sooner or later, he'll have reason to be in America and he'll find a way to finish this job."

Marina crossed her arms against another chill. "Then what can we do?"

"Work with us to stop him now."

DAVID WATCHED AS MARINA paced to the door and checked through the peephole for what was probably the tenth time in the past hour. He couldn't fault her for that. If he'd been more mobile, he'd probably be doing the same. He propped his crutches against the armchair where he'd left his suit coat, then lowered himself to the sofa. It was well after midnight, and they'd dimmed most of the lights, leaving only one lamp on a side table burning, but he doubted that either he or Marina would feel like sleeping anytime soon. "Are the guards still there?" he asked.

She nodded. "Do you think two are enough?"

"Gideon told me the penthouse deck was designed to accommodate high-profile clients who often need extra security. The largest suites like this one are the most secure, so Stefan will be safer right here than anywhere else." He tugged off his tie, rolled it into a ball and tossed it toward his jacket. "I can't thank you enough for offering to let us stay with you. I realize it's an imposition on your privacy."

"Don't be absurd," she said, glancing at him over her shoulder. "I have far more room than I need, and this concerns me as much as you. Fedorovich murdered my sister."

"I'm truly sorry, Marina."

"So am I. It wasn't fair. Borya's only crime was being a good man." She flattened her hands on the door and returned her attention to the peephole. "They would want us to do this. Fedorovich must be stopped."

"He will be. Now that the ship's security personnel know what he looks like, if by some fluke he does get on board, he won't get near us."

"Stefan said he saw him in the Empire Room tonight. He could already be here."

It was a switch for David to be the one being reasonable about this instead of Marina, but now that they knew for certain what they were dealing with, he found it easier to think clearly. They were no longer battling a phantom. Stefan's monster had a face and a name, and trained law enforcement agents were helping them fight it. "The possibility of Fedorovich getting on board is remote. I think Gideon assigned those guards to us more for our peace of mind than anything else." David also suspected the guards were Gideon's way of apologizing for his earlier skepticsm. "We both know Fedorovich couldn't have been there every time Stefan told us he saw his monster."

"Yes, but how can we be sure?"

He could see how upset she was, so he spared her the explanation. From what Locatelli had told him about Fedorovich's ruthlessness, if the hit man had gotten that close to them, chances were Stefan would already be dead. "All we can do is stay put and let the experts do their jobs," he said.

She shoved away from the door and paced across the living room. "I could hire extra security people to patrol the Palermo harbor. Or I could post rewards."

"If you do that, it could warn Fedorovich off. There would be no telling when he'd show up again."

"God, I hate feeling helpless!"

David moved a throw cushion from the sofa to the coffee table in front of him, then eased his bad leg on top of it. He hated feeling helpless, too, he thought, adjusting the cushion so that his knee was supported. Of all the times to be out of commission with a sprain.

"The man truly must be a monster." Marina stopped beside the balcony doors and pressed her nose to the glass to peer outside. "How could he want to hurt a child?"

"Who knows what makes anyone want to do that?"

She whirled from the glass to look at him. "Oh, David, I'm sorry. I didn't think."

"What?"

She strode to the sofa. "You know about monsters who hurt children. I should have believed you. You saw the truth all along."

"I can't take credit for that, Marina. I was seeing myself

in Stefan and jumped to the wrong conclusion. I was completely off base."

"You had the facts wrong, but you got the important part right. You weren't using this," she said, placing two fingers against his forehead. She moved her hand to his chest and tapped her fingers over his heart. "You used this. You trusted your instincts. That's how you knew Stefan was in trouble. And thank God you did. Otherwise…"

David slid his hand over hers to hold it against his chest. He'd lost track of the number of times they'd touched each other since they'd come back to her stateroom. It seemed pointless to fight it—she probably needed this as much as he did.

Her chin trembled. "My poor, sweet Stefan. All those months he spent in the orphanages, he was keeping this nightmare inside. You helped him when no one else would."

"I felt a bond with Stefan from the moment I saw him on the adoption video."

"And this was why. Your heart recognized it."

"Maybe it did."

She blinked hard, chewing on her lower lip.

He rubbed her knuckles. "What?" he asked.

"When I heard you had adopted Stefan, I hated you."

"Sure. I can understand that."

"No, really, *really* hated you. I called you a thief and a kidnapper and wanted you to disappear. Rudolph had even worried that I might try to throw you overboard. But if you hadn't been the one to adopt Stefan…" Her eyelashes sparkled with tears. "If no one had believed him or had made the police look for his nightmare monster, he would have been completely defenseless. No one would have known he *needed* defending. There would be nothing to stop Fedorovich from finishing his job." She shook her head, knocking the last coil of hair from its gold clip to tumble around her face. "I'm glad it was you, David."

The scent of apples stole over him, as welcome as the warmth of her hand against his chest. He inhaled slowly. "Want to know what I thought when I heard Stefan's maiden aunt had filed a claim for him?"

"You hated me, too."

"No, my reaction wasn't that strong, because I hadn't taken you seriously. I thought you were some elderly, dried-up spinster who didn't care about Stefan but was going through the motions to soothe her conscience."

She withdrew her hand from his. "Didn't care?"

Incredibly he felt a smile tighten his cheeks. That was just like Marina. She hadn't taken exception to being called elderly or dried-up, but she wouldn't tolerate anyone casting doubt on her love for her nephew. "It took me less than a day to figure out I was wrong," he said.

"I do care. I would do anything for him."

He reached up to catch a lock of her hair. "That's true. You were willing to send him to America with me."

"Only to keep him safe, David."

"Yes, I got that."

"And I might be grateful that it was *you* who adopted him but that doesn't mean I'm glad he was adopted. I still want to take him home with me."

"Yes, I understand that, too." He spread his fingers to let her hair slide through them. "Given the circumstances, do you think we could shelve the custody debate for a while?"

She wiped her eyes with the back of her hand, then sighed, walked around the coffee table and sat beside him on the sofa. She took out her empty hair clip and snapped it together in her fingers a few times. "This is my fault."

"Why?"

"I should have tried harder to find Stefan. There must have been something else I could have done."

"It sounds as if you did all you could."

"I shouldn't have gone to Paris that August. Or I should have convinced Borya and Olena to move to Moscow. None of this would have happened if they hadn't stayed in Murmansk."

"Don't blame yourself, Marina. You can't control what other people do."

"I know. It's just that when I think of how easily Stefan could have been…" She dropped her hair clip on the table, then pulled her feet onto the sofa and wrapped her arms around her legs. "The thought of losing him makes me crazy. That child is all I have left."

He draped his arm along the sofa back, angling his shoulders so he could regard her. She'd discarded her shoes as soon as Gideon and Captain Locatelli had departed—her bare feet peeked from beneath the hem of the shimmery dress she'd worn to dinner. The fabric was stretched taut over her thighs as she curled up the way Stefan did when he was anxious.

Despite all her wealth and the flamboyant self-confidence she carried herself with, at this moment she looked lost. Alone. It was how she'd looked the first night of the cruise, when she'd stood between the twin beds in his stateroom and had watched Stefan sleep.

Marina had told him more than once that she had no desire to get married, and that she'd been too focused on her career to consider having a family. David had been too eager to use those points in his favor to really examine them before.

Something didn't add up. She was a passionate woman, yet she had no boyfriend. She loved her nephew fiercely, yet she had chosen a life without children.

He moved his hand to her shoulder. "What's the real reason you never got married, Marina?"

"What? I told you, it wasn't for me."

"Yes, you told me about wanting to create beauty because of dark winters and wanting more from life than Murmansk could offer you, but I've seen how you feel about Stefan. I can't believe you never wanted a family of your own."

She tilted her head, sending a lock of hair sliding across his hand. "I didn't say I never wanted it, David, only that I accepted it wasn't for me."

"What does that mean?"

"I knew I would never be like Olena. She got the best of both of our parents. She inherited our father's charm and our mother's beauty. Every boy in school couldn't help but fall in love with her."

He reversed his hand to finger the ends of her hair. "What did that have to do with you?"

"I grew up seeing the contrast. It made me look for other things to value."

"I still don't understand. What contrast?"

She rolled her eyes and waved her hand at her face.

"What?"

"Surely you've noticed my nose."

"There's nothing wrong with your nose."

"No, aside from the fact there's an overabundance of it, it functions perfectly well. But imagine this nose on the face of a five-year-old, along with these ears," she said, grasping her hair from his hand to hold it out from the side of her head.

"There's nothing wrong with your ears, either. They're like Stefan's."

"Of course there's nothing wrong with them. Not to an adult, but when I was a child, I could have been mistaken for a milk jug." She flipped her hair over her shoulder. "Now, picture a tall, skinny adolescent having to wear the dresses that had looked so wonderful on her voluptuous older sister. I couldn't complain, because our family wasn't rich and those clothes were good, but there were hurtful comparisons whenever Olena and I went anywhere together."

"That's when you started your designing," he said. "You told me you learned to alter Olena's hand-me-downs."

"Yes, that's when it started. I didn't have the power to change how *I* looked, but I did have the power to make the clothes look beautiful. Because I knew my work was good, I wouldn't abide any more jokes at the expense of my appearance, so whenever one of Olena's friends made an unkind comment, I learned to fling the comment right back."

"I can see that," he said. "You still don't let anyone push you around."

"My sister warned me against speaking my mind. She claimed I'd never get a boyfriend that way, but I never considered trying to acquire one. I found my designs far more interesting than the men who swarmed around her."

"What about later, after you moved to Moscow? Did you ever wonder if you were missing something?"

She shifted to lean into the corner of the sofa, drawing away from his touch. "Not at first. My work really did keep me too busy. I didn't spare the time for romance."

"Never?"

She slanted a look at him. "I'm thirty-two years old, David. I am not a virgin. I just haven't met a man who held my interest for long."

If she'd been a different woman, he might have taken that remark as a sexual challenge. But he knew Marina hadn't meant it that way. She was simply being honest, as she always was. "And once the Artamova label became successful," he said, filling in her story, "you suspected men were attracted to your bank account, right?"

"Exactly."

"That's harsh."

"That's the advantage of growing up ugly," she said. "One learns to look for the truth beneath the surface."

There was pride in her voice, not self-pity, so he bit back the automatic denial he'd wanted to make. He'd always thought she was beautiful, yet he realized that her beauty didn't arise from her features. It was a product of her energy and her passion, and her irrepressible emotions. Beauty shone from the way she angled her chin and looked him square in the eyes, refusing to back down when she believed she was right. He smiled and leaned closer so he could run his fingertip along the rim of her ear. "You're gorgeous now," he said. "You must know that."

"Thank you. It's what I do for a living. I design clothes that can make any woman look beautiful." She pinched one of the creases of fabric where her dress folded behind her bent knees. "I use color and cut to emphasize a woman's good points and minimize the bad, then I put the garment together with a fabric that is comfortable to wear. This one's stretchy. It's one of our highest sellers."

David moved his gaze from her knee to her thigh. She seemed to believe it was only her clothes that made her attractive, but that was nonsense. She would look even better naked.

He tried to ignore the jump of his pulse that followed that thought. There were security men outside the door, he reminded himself. There was a ruthless killer waiting at the next port for his son. He should think of something besides how enticing the curve of Marina's hip looked.

She grasped her hem and gave it a sharp tug over her ankles. "But to answer your question, yes, I've always known I was missing something. I don't possess a fraction of the maternal instincts Olena had, yet when I first saw her hold her newborn son, my arms felt so empty, they ached."

"Yet you didn't change your mind about romance."

"I can't change who I am, David. I'm short-tempered and opinionated, I have no patience for courtship rituals and I spend most of my waking hours working. Whether or not I wanted a love like Olena and Borya were blessed with, and a baby of my own to cherish, it wasn't going to happen. I've accepted the fact that my path was decided decades ago."

"Marina…"

"And that's why I can't let anything happen to Stefan." She dropped her forehead to her knees. "Without him, I am completely alone."

David didn't stop to think this time. He wrapped his arms around her and pulled her to his chest.

She held herself stiffly. "David, we agreed not to—"

"I just want to hold you," he said. "That's all."

"You'd better not be feeling sorry for me."

"Hell, no. I'd sooner feel sorry for those men who wanted to date you and found out how short-tempered and opinionated you are."

"I shouldn't have told you that."

"It's not as if I hadn't already noticed, Marina. You're not the easiest person in the world to get along with."

"Well, you're aggravating."

"True, but I also feel like holding you."

Sighing, she lowered her knees and curled her legs on the cushion beneath her, her body relaxing as she snuggled to his side. "You are still my enemy, David," she said, leaning her head on his shoulder.

"Yes." He stroked her hair, marveling at how naturally she fit against him. "And you're mine."

"As soon as Fedorovich is caught, our debate is back on."

"Absolutely."

"Because Stefan belongs with me."

"Enough," he said, moving his hand to her mouth to stop her from making any further comments.

But he should have known that Marina wouldn't be silenced if she chose not to be. She closed her teeth over the side of his finger and bit down lightly on his knuckle.

The sensation of her teeth on his skin wreaked havoc on his good intentions. He caught her chin to tip up her face.

She splayed her fingers over his chest, a defiant gleam in her eyes. She parted her lips, but instead of speaking, she dropped her gaze to his mouth.

David was not sure who moved first. He lowered his head as she was lifting hers. Their mouths met with a force that bordered on painful, but neither of them backed down. He grasped the nape of her neck as she cupped the back of his head, each holding the other in place. It was a kiss of frustration and of challenge. It only ended when they ran out of breath.

She pressed her cheek to his, gasping for air. "I don't want to kiss you again, David."

"I know you don't," he said. He eased her mouth back to his. "Hell of a situation, isn't it?"

This time, the kiss began with her laughter. David could feel it in the tremor that tightened her lips and jiggled her breast against his side. He let go of her nape to move his hand down her shoulder. The caress blended so easily into their kiss, he hadn't realized he'd cupped her breast in his palm until she pulled back to look down at his hand.

Keeping his gaze on her face, he rubbed his thumb across the fabric that covered her nipple.

Her eyes darkened. The tremor that went through her breast this time wasn't from laughter.

"I lied, Marina," he murmured. "I want to do more than hold you."

CHAPTER ELEVEN

IT WAS MADNESS. Stupidity. It could only end badly.

Yet at this moment, Marina could think of nothing she wanted more. The invitation in David's eyes, and the sensation of his hand precisely where she longed to feel it, were more than she could resist. She leaned into his caress, opened the buttons on his shirt and slipped her hands inside.

Had it only been two days since she'd laid her hands on his bare chest? It seemed like forever, or like minutes ago. The time that had passed had no meaning as she felt the heat of his skin beneath her palms.

His body was magnificent, she thought, sliding her fingers along the smooth swell of his muscles. She loved the masculine textures, the tautness of his skin, the soft brush of his hair as it sprang back against her fingertips. She loved the strength that hummed through his frame, even when he was at rest.

"Hang on," he whispered, clamping one arm behind her back. He released her breast and braced his hand on the cushions, holding her securely as he shifted beneath her. Keeping one foot on the floor, he twisted sideways to bring his injured leg on the sofa, then leaned back against the side so she could stretch out on top of him.

Oh, yes, he was strong, she thought, enjoying the flexing

that was going on beneath her. And it felt wonderful to be held by a man who was taller than her. He was resourceful, too. Even with one knee wrapped in a bandage and bruises over most of his right side...

She slid backward quickly until she was kneeling on the cushion in the V of his legs.

He grasped her upper arms, stopping her from retreating further. "What's wrong?"

"I should keep my weight off you." She ran her palm along his right thigh. "I don't want to hurt you."

"You won't." He tugged her forward to lie on top of him again. "Now, where were we?"

Marina shifted her hands to the sofa arm behind him to hold herself off his chest, doing her best to spare him her full weight.

He caught her hair in his hand as it swung forward and brought it to his nose. His eyes half closed as he inhaled. Somehow, the gesture seemed more intimate than when he'd caressed her breast.

Smiling, she dipped her head between her arms to bring her nose to the side of his neck and drew in the scent of his skin. It was tart, pleasantly musky, a blend of soap and pine and something she knew was simply David.

Yet there was nothing simple about David, was there? Each day she spent with him revealed more. She could spend a lifetime with him and still not get enough.

Marina's fingernails dug into the leather of the sofa arm. A lifetime? No, they had only two more days. Less than that, because any minute one of them was going to come to their senses. She pressed her lips to the hollow at the base of his throat. She could feel his pulse there, its beat as headlong and heedless as hers.

This was going to hurt, no matter how careful they both tried to be....

Cool air touched her back. David had found the hidden closure at the back of her dress and was lowering her zipper. She could feel the fabric loosening, falling away from her sides. He peeled it off her shoulders until it caught at her elbows.

She kissed the ridge of a tendon beneath his ear and hung on to the sofa, waiting, her breathing shallow, her pulse racing. He was going to stop, she told herself. He was the sensible one, the logical one, not her.

Yet he didn't stop. He stroked the small of her back, then slipped his hands inside her dress to run his knuckles along her bare midriff. His thumb traced the lower edge of her bra, his touch as gentle as if they had all night.

But it wasn't gentleness she wanted, because that would give her time to think. She sat back on her heels to free her arms from her sleeves and shimmied her dress to her waist. Then she shrugged off her bra and rocked forward on her knees to return her mouth to David's.

Although he was beneath her, he took charge of the kiss, using his tongue, his teeth and the power of his hands on her body to position her where he wanted. Marina shuddered as he smoothed his palms down her hips to cup her buttocks. With each caress, each squeeze, the rivalry that had been sparking between them for more than a week was transforming into desire.

She loved the way he touched her. He was using his strength for her pleasure, making her body hum with need. And she wasn't the only one. She could feel him swell and harden beneath her. It seemed so right, she wished she could forget who he was and just enjoy the moment. If only she could pretend he was someone else, that they were merely a man and a woman, sharing the mindless comfort of sex.

But she knew that some other man wouldn't make her feel this good. Because no other man was David. And no one else had worked his way into her heart the way he had....

No! She didn't want to think.

Yet the truth was there in the tingles that followed his touch, in the heat that flowed from his kiss. The pleasure came from a source far deeper than the skin he stroked. It came from the way he looked at her, and from the way he listened as if he cared. It had been building from the moment she'd seen those marks on his back and had understood how he'd become the man he was. No, it had started earlier than that, when she'd seen the tenderness in his smile and glimpsed the passion behind his amber gaze. How could she help falling in love....

No!

She broke off the kiss, nosed aside his shirt and grazed the edges of her teeth across his collarbone. This couldn't be love. It wasn't possible. This man wanted to take her nephew away. She wasn't about to hand him her heart, too.

He moved his hands to her hips, his grasp no longer gentle. "Marina?"

Her pulse was pounding so hard, it took her a moment before she heard the cry. She jerked her head up.

The cry came again, louder than before and high-pitched with panic.

David reacted faster than she did. She had barely managed to push herself off him when he jackknifed from the sofa, grabbed one of his crutches and vaulted toward the bedroom door. "Stefan!"

Marina tried to follow but her dress tangled around her ankles, sending her crashing into the coffee table.

The lock on the suite door clicked an instant before the door swung open. The two security guards who had been in the corridor raced into the living room, their weapons drawn.

Marina pointed to the bedroom. David had already disappeared inside. "In there!" she cried. "My nephew."

One of the men ran forward, but the other hesitated, his gaze on her breasts.

Marina swore in Russian and yanked up her dress while she got to her feet. Whether or not the man understood what she'd called him, he got back to business and did a swift survey of the living area and the dining room before he advanced to the bedroom doorway. Marina was right on his heels but he held out his arm to bar her way. "Ma'am, you'd better keep back."

She shoved her arms into her sleeves and reached behind her back to do up her zipper as she peered past him.

David had switched on the bedside lamp and was sitting on the edge of the bed with Stefan on his lap. The other guard was looking out the bedroom window, his weapon pointed to the ceiling. There was no sign of an intruder, nothing out of place except the sheets that lay twisted in the center of the mattress.

"False alarm," the guard said, turning away from the glass. "There's nothing out there."

"All clear in here, as well."

Marina ducked beneath the man's arm and went to kneel beside David. She stroked Stefan's back. "Stefochka, what's wrong?"

"He had another nightmare," David answered.

Stefan sucked hard on his thumb as he looked at Marina.

His other hand was clasped around the edge of David's open shirtfront.

"He was pointing at the window," David continued. "He thought the monster was outside."

Marina sprang back to her feet and went around the bed to the window. "Look again," she told the guard, cupping her hands around her eyes so she could look past the reflection in the glass.

"There's no one out there," he said. "There couldn't be."

Logically, she knew he was right. All she could see were stars glittering on the sea. The veranda didn't extend in front of the bedroom, so Stefan *couldn't* have seen anyone out there. It wouldn't be reasonable to carry the search further, yet for Stefan's sake, she wanted to be sure. "You," she ordered, turning to point at the guard in the doorway. "Go outside and check the veranda."

"Miss, it's a waste of time."

She propped her hands on her hips. "You already wasted enough time looking at my breasts. Do you consider them more of a threat than a Russian hit man?"

A dull red suffused the skin above his white collar. He turned away without another word.

Twenty minutes later the entire suite, including the bathrooms and the veranda, had been searched to Marina's satisfaction, but no trace of anyone else could be found. Only then did she agree that it had indeed been a false alarm. She closed the door behind the guards, watching through the peephole to make sure they had resumed their posts, then turned and leaned her back against the door.

The coffee table was still askew where she'd knocked into it. David's jacket and tie were draped over an armchair and her hair clip and bra were lying on the carpet.

She stared at the reminders of what she and David had been doing. It all looked too ordinary compared to the problem of a hit man on the loose, yet to her it carried its own kind of threat. She had been on the verge of making love with David. Worse, she was on the verge of falling in love.

It was just as well they'd been interrupted before either one of those disasters had gone to its completion.

David was tucking the coverlet around Stefan's shoulders as she returned to the bedroom. He straightened up from the bed and placed his finger against his lips.

She stopped just inside the doorway. "Is he all right?" she whispered.

David nodded. "He seems okay." He switched off the bedside light, fitted his crutch under his arm and moved to her side. As she'd seen him do in his own stateroom, he'd left the light in the bathroom on and the door ajar so the room wasn't completely dark. "I think Stefan's feeling better now that he can see we're all believing him," he said quietly.

"The guards didn't find anyone."

"I didn't expect them to. Stefan used half English and half Russian when he told me about the monster this time, so I was able to understand what he said. This was definitely only a dream." He nodded his chin toward the window. "He told me it was raining."

She looked at the pinpricks of stars beyond the glass, then thought about the cause of Stefan's nightmares. "It was raining the night of the accident."

"He's remembering more details."

"I don't know whether or not that's good. It's going to upset him."

"I'll talk to a specialist when we get home. Now that we

know the source of Stefan's anxieties, I can work out the best way to handle them."

She crossed her arms and watched her nephew sleep for a while, reassuring herself with the sound of his steady breathing. David stood silently at her side, close enough for her to feel the heat of his body, but she didn't touch him or lean into him the way she longed to. The issue of who got Stefan was once more between them.

When we get home. He had meant Stefan and himself, of course. She wasn't included.

Not that she expected to be. David might know what she smelled like, and he might remember how her tongue had felt sliding against his lips, but nothing had really changed. It was clear he had his priorities straight. She should, too.

David brought his head next to hers. "Marina, about what happened earlier…"

"It was just a few kisses, David. Not a big deal. I'm not going to apologize."

His breath warmed her ear. "Neither am I."

"And you don't have to tell me it can't happen again. I know that. I was just feeling…alone."

"I understand." He put his finger beneath her jaw and turned her face toward his. "I want you to sleep in here with Stefan tonight."

"No, I was going to let the two of you have the bedroom. That sofa in the living room folds out to a bed."

"Sleep here, Marina. I'll take the sofa."

"It's shorter than this bed and I'm not as tall as you. I don't have a sprained knee, either."

"The knee's getting better. I can hardly feel it."

"Do you always have to prove how gallant you are?"

"Do you always have to argue?"

"David…"

He nudged her chin upward and kissed her.

It was only a brief swoop of his mouth over hers, a mere aftertaste of the kisses he'd given her earlier, but within seconds she was swaying toward him.

She caught the edge of the door frame to stay where she was.

David put his hand over hers. "I'm not gallant, Marina," he whispered. "I want you to sleep in Stefan's bed so I won't be as tempted to sleep in yours."

MARINA SLASHED THE pencil across her sketchbook, carving a groove into the paper. Instead of discarding the page, she turned the deep line into a set of square shoulders, then added more lines to suggest flowing sleeves. She pictured the garment made up in a soft fabric, something that wouldn't create bulk where it was gathered yet would still be firm enough to accentuate the attractive angle where the torso met the hips. She could see it in natural linen, fine-woven and washed into pliability. An understated color. More angles in the yoke to accommodate broad shoulders…

She halted, her pencil poised in midstroke. This was a man's shirt. She didn't design men's clothing.

Gritting her teeth, she flipped to a clean page. The sketchbook had been her last resort. She'd already gone through every fax that Siiri had sent her and had spent hours on the phone sorting through the problems that had been stacking up at her office. She needed to focus on something other than the endless waiting, and it was usually easy to get lost in her work. It was something familiar, the one thing she knew she was good at. It was how she filled her life.

Yet it was proving to be no source of comfort today. Thoughts of David were invading even this. Her lips could still feel his kiss as clearly as the fresh page of her sketchbook bore the impression of her pencil.

Damn the man. She did not want to think about him. She'd done enough of that the night before. What kind of aunt was she, to be wasting any time worrying about her own feelings when a hit man who wanted to kill her nephew was stalking the ship?

She slammed the sketchbook on the dining table and rose to her feet. "Have you heard anything yet, Officer Gallo?"

The young man who stood beside the veranda door pressed his index finger to his earpiece and shook his head. "No, Miss Artamova. Still no developments."

She went to look through the glass. The hills beyond the harbor were already darkening with dusk. Lights glowed from the buildings that lined the waterfront and from the upper story of the cruise terminal on the pier where the ship was moored. She couldn't see the pier itself from inside her stateroom, nor could she see any patrol cars or other signs of police presence around the harbor, but Locatelli had assured her the entire area was under close surveillance.

She glanced at the guard who was stationed beside the suite's entrance. There were still two guards from the ship's security force outside in the corridor, but the men in here were plainclothes policemen. They'd positioned themselves inside the suite when *Alexandra's Dream* had docked in Palermo and had remained here since then. They appeared content to wait.

So did David. He'd been the epitome of control all day, the perfect parent in his bland golf shirt. Except for a quick trip to his stateroom to pick up clean clothes and a bag of Stefan's toys, he hadn't left the penthouse.

Stefan had taken his cue from David and had been surprisingly calm about his confinement, and about their silent bodyguards. Whenever he'd become restless, David had done his best to distract the child with music or video games. They were currently sitting on the living room floor together, Stefan already bathed and dressed in his Spider-Man pajamas. He had been adding pieces to the boat they'd made out of small, brightly colored building blocks. It looked more like a tiny, lop-sided bathtub than a boat—Marina wouldn't have known what it was supposed to be if David hadn't told her.

But Stefan wasn't paying attention to the boat anymore; he was watching Marina, his eyebrows angled together beneath his wispy blond bangs.

This was why she'd picked up her sketchbook in the first place. It was the reason she'd kept herself busy with her work. She'd realized her anxiousness was upsetting Stefan and she hadn't wanted to inflict her mood on him. Whenever she'd gone near him, she'd ended up holding him too tightly or too long until he'd squirmed to get away. She forced her cheeks into a smile and blew him a kiss, then turned so that her nephew wouldn't be able to see her face as she addressed the guard again. "Tell Captain Locatelli that I'm going for a walk on the pier."

He frowned. "That's not a good idea, Miss Artamova."

She gestured toward the darkening sky. "We're due to sail in less than an hour and Fedorovich hasn't turned up. I could draw him out."

"How?"

"He saw me with David and Stefan in Naples, so when

he sees me alone now he would think I'm going to meet them. He might come out from wherever he's hiding to follow me. It's worth a try."

He appeared to consider that for a while. "I appreciate your desire to assist us, but it would be better if you remain here with your nephew and Mr. Anderson."

"We all thought this would be over by now, but it's not. I can no longer sit and do nothing. You need bait, Officer Gallo. I can be bait."

He shook his head. "We would need to fit you with communication devices. You would also need to wear a bulletproof vest."

She flicked her fingers. "That would waste too much time. I won't go far."

"You'd better discuss this with Captain Locatelli before you do anything."

She suspected Locatelli wouldn't agree to her plan any more than David would, so she had no intention of discussing it with either man. "Am I under arrest?"

"Well, no, but—"

"Then you can't really stop me from taking a walk, can you?"

"Fedorovich has killed two men that we know of in his attempt to reach your nephew. If you insist on doing this, we won't be able to guarantee your safety."

"It's not my safety I'm concerned about," she said. She glanced over her shoulder. Stefan and David were both on their knees as they pushed the boat along the carpet on a voyage around the furniture.

It was another one of those snapshot images that would probably stay in her memory forever. Their features were nothing alike. David's eyes were warm amber and Stefan's were pale blue. David's hair was thick and dark brown while Stefan's was fine blond. They were from different backgrounds, different cultures, yet they looked like father and son, as if they belonged together....

And that's when it finally struck her. Stefan turned to David when he had a bad dream. He looked to David for guidance and approval. It was David he ran to first, David who understood his needs. The instinctive bond David had felt with Stefan, the recognition that had saved the child's life, must have worked both ways.

The truth was right in front of her. While Marina had been trying hard not to fall in love with David, Stefan already had.

God, this just kept getting worse.

CHAPTER TWELVE

ILYA REMAINED MOTIONLESS as another security guard walked past, but the man didn't glance in his direction. No one expected to see him here. They were concentrating on the pier and the Palermo cruise terminal, just as they had since the ship had arrived in Sicily this morning. Ilya had had no trouble spotting the Italian police who had taken up positions around the harbor. They'd disguised themselves as tourists and likely thought he wouldn't notice them, yet he'd learned long ago how to spot his enemy. The fools thought they would trap him, but they were all looking in the wrong place.

A flash of red near the taxi stand beside the terminal building caught his eye. Ilya pressed closer to the ship's railing, squinting to focus his gaze as he watched the Artamova woman arguing with the policeman who had been shadowing her. No doubt she was trying to refuse his order to return to the ship. If Ilya had been capable of laughter, he would have been amused by their last-minute attempt to draw him into the open. She had been wandering around the pier for the past half hour, her strategy pathetically transparent, a product of frustration rather than reasoning. Whoever was running this operation would never have survived in a real battle.

That was why Ilya would prevail. He could be frustrated by the setbacks he'd encountered on this job, but he wouldn't let that interfere with his duty. He looked at his watch. Only minutes were left before the ship sailed. The authorities would realize their trap had failed and would be scurrying to regroup. But they wouldn't be looking for him when the ship stopped in Malta tomorrow. Ilya had already arranged for Sergei to send them elsewhere with a simple phone call.

Yes, plenty of people relied on that Moscow doorman for information, even the police.

Keeping his gaze on the red-clad Artamova, Ilya repositioned himself in a less well-illuminated area of the deck. It was unfortunate the priest he had seen in Alghero hadn't been taller—dressing as a member of the clergy would have been excellent camouflage. Still, the deckhand Ilya had selected from among the people who had been returning to the ship had been close to his size and bearded, which was even better. Best of all, he'd bled like a slaughtered pig.

For a moment the red of Artamova's dress blended with Ilya's memory of the blood pool that had spread around his feet. The deckhand's death had been a good one. Ilya had placed the bullets carefully to maximize the time it would take. The man had almost lasted long enough to ease the ache....

Almost.

He gnawed the inside of his cheek, steadying himself with the taste of blood. The ID he'd taken from the body had been good enough to get him on board, but it wouldn't have stood up to the scrutiny of the heightened security measures that had been implemented today.

It had been a mistake to rely on Misha. The Russian crewman had obviously warned someone about Ilya's target. Or perhaps someone had recognized him in Naples. Regardless, no one should recognize him now. Although Ilya disliked the sensation of having anything on his face, donning the fake beard was often necessary when he needed to blend in with a crowd.

And his strategy was working superbly. As soon as he'd gotten on board, he had scouted the territory to familiarize himself with the layout of the ship. Once he'd noted the security patrols and the locations of the surveillance cameras, it had been easy to work out the best routes to use in order to get around unnoticed. A brief visit to the ship's laundry service had provided him with clothes that allowed him to blend in with the passengers, giving him the freedom to move almost anywhere unquestioned.

Yet the moment Ilya had entered the dining room yesterday, the boy had spotted him and dived under the table.

That should have been only a temporary setback. From there, Ilya had gone straight to Anderson's stateroom to wait for the man and boy to return. He'd intended to kill them both in their beds, the way he'd first planned when Misha had given him the passenger list. He'd waited until after midnight for them to show up before he'd gone to check Artamova's penthouse.

He'd hoped for a swift end then, too. He'd expected to find Anderson coupling with the woman—a better use for her than the quarreling he'd witnessed in Naples. With the adults distracted it should have been simple to eliminate all three.

Instead he'd found armed security men in the corridor.

He slipped his hand into his pants pocket and stroked the

barrel of his gun. He'd anticipated this kill too many times now. His need to finish was becoming more urgent. The child's continued existence was an affront to Ilya's skills.

But no mere boy was going to thwart Colonel Ilya Fedorovich. It was going to end tonight. He would dispose of the bodies at sea and tomorrow he would blend in with the passengers and walk away. That should be simple—the authorities were so confident in their own infallibility, they were concentrating their scrutiny on people who boarded the ship, not those who were leaving.

Keeping his face averted from the cameras on the deck and in the elevator, he made his way down to the hotel lobby and walked toward the flow of returning passengers. It was obliging of Artamova to wear red. It would make her easy to pick out among the stragglers.

MIKE MOISTENED HIS LIPS as he glanced into the Emperor's Club. Some refreshment at the ship's wine bar would help take the edge off his nerves, but he had more urgent business to attend to. He spotted Giorgio near the elevators and changed course to intercept him. "I noticed some plainclothes cops were staking out the cruise terminal when I got back," he said. "What's going on?"

For a change, Giorgio wasn't watching the ladies, he was watching a pair of men in sport coats who were walking past the bar. He caught Mike's elbow and detoured into the corridor that ran through the deck. "We've got trouble. Did you make the pickup?"

That didn't help Mike's nerves. He needed a drink more than ever now. He pasted on the Father Connelly smile for the benefit of any passengers who were strolling nearby and tightened his grasp on the package he held against his chest. "One Hellenistic fish plate, first century B.C. It went without a hitch."

"Give it to me. I'll get rid of it."

"I've got a fake receipt."

"That's not good enough. The police aren't only on the dock, they're here."

"Here? You mean, on board? Why?"

"They were tipped off by Interpol."

Mike's palms started to sweat. He eased his free hand along the side of his pants to dry it. Interpol could disseminate information to every police agency in the region. Once they got on the scent, trouble couldn't be left behind simply by sailing to the next port. "I thought the boss had connections. We should have been warned."

"The boss might not have heard about it. Word is it's got something to do with that boy whose father got hit by a car. You've probably seen them around. Little blond kid with a big guy on crutches."

Mike immediately knew who Giorgio meant. Even among a thousand passengers, a pair like that stood out. "Right. They're usually with that tall, blond woman."

"From what I heard, a hit man from the Russian mob is after them. Ship's security is on high alert."

"Oh, hell."

"Yeah." Giorgio looked over his shoulder, then paused near the entrance to the library where there were fewer people. "If the police decide to do a sweep of the ship—"

"The goods are safe in my collection. The cops would be looking for a hit man, not smugglers."

"So they say."

"You sound as if you don't believe them."

"What if the hit man story is only a smokescreen and

they really are looking for contraband? I don't want to risk screwing this up on the first sailing of the summer. I already took the stuff out of your cabin. I'll get rid of it with that plate. We can pick up extra to make up for it."

"*We?* I'm the one doing the legwork."

"And it's my job to make sure the goods make it to our buyer. Your idea of keeping them in plain sight was dumb to begin with. You've got no deniability if they're found on you."

Mike's gaze strayed to the library. "I have pieces from my collection in plain sight every time I do a lecture."

"You haven't used any of the real ones yet, have you?"

"No, but maybe I should get the ship to keep them for me."

"Don't get cute, Mike," Giorgio muttered, turning away. "If you're caught, you're on your own."

DAVID LOOKED AT HIS watch, then hobbled to the veranda where Locatelli was conversing with one of the men who had been guarding the suite. The hell with being patient. The ship had left the harbor thirty minutes ago. Full darkness had already fallen, yet Marina still hadn't returned. "What's going on?" David demanded. "Where is she?"

Locatelli held up one finger as he pressed a walkie-talkie to his ear. He listened for a few seconds, then turned to David. The light that spilled through the open door accentuated the weathered lines on his face, strengthening his resemblance to a bulldog. "We still haven't located her."

"How can you lose track of a woman like Marina? She was wearing red. You could spot her a mile away."

"Mr. Anderson…"

"You should have ordered the captain to wait. She might still be in Palermo."

"No, the officer who was assigned to her confirmed that he escorted her back to the ship. He didn't lose track of her until after we'd embarked."

"How did that happen? He's a trained policeman. She designs women's fashions."

"Apparently there was a disturbance in the lobby. Someone had reported finding some Greek artifacts in a potted plant. We'll need to do tests to determine whether they're the real thing, but if they're genuine, there could be a smuggler on board."

David ground his teeth. "You were telling me about Marina?"

"While our officer paused to deal with the artifacts, Miss Artamova went to help a young woman with a baby stroller and then just slipped away. It's possible that she decided she needed some time to herself and simply chose to go for a walk before she returns."

Yes, he knew that was possible. Anything was possible with Marina. She was impulsive and headstrong. He'd seen how difficult their confinement had been on her. She'd been a bundle of nerves all day.

But he'd known some of her tension was from more than the issue of Fedorovich. It was from what had almost happened between them the night before.

She hadn't touched David since then. She hadn't met his gaze, either. He'd tried telling himself that was for the best, but damn it, he'd gotten used to her company. He wanted her with him, even if it was only to argue.

He raked his hand through his hair, striving for control, but he was fighting a losing battle. His calm had deserted him the moment he'd realized that Marina had put herself in danger. He turned his gaze on Officer

Gallo. "She shouldn't have been allowed out of the suite in the first place."

Gallo cleared his throat. "Miss Artamova was very insistent about helping. I couldn't have legally stopped her."

"Then you should have told me what she was planning. I would have stopped her even if I'd had to drag her back from the door and sit on her."

"Officer Gallo is not at fault," Locatelli said. "In principle, Miss Artamova's idea of drawing Fedorovich out was worth a try. She was observed constantly, and we knew she wasn't the target."

"Sure, but—"

"This point isn't worth pursuing, Mr. Anderson. Regardless of Miss Artamova's efforts, it seems as if our operation here might have been in vain from the beginning."

"What do you mean?"

"Mr. Dayan has just relayed some new information from the Russian authorities," he said, indicating the walkie-talkie he'd been listening to earlier. "One of their informants in Moscow claims Fedorovich arrived there this morning. It appears as if he already realized he would not gain access to the boy during this cruise."

David couldn't be happy about that. It might mean the immediate threat had eased, but Stefan was far from safe. "What happens now?"

"We'll continue to provide your son protection for the time being. However, when you return to America, that will be up to the FBI and your local authorities in Burlington."

It was the worst-case scenario. How could he take his new son home and give him a normal life if that murderer was still on the loose? And what about the rest of the Anderson family, and David's students? Fedorovich had already killed in his attempts to get to Stefan. No one who was near him would be safe. David fisted his hands. If he'd been capable of it, he would have kicked something.

The phone rang in the suite. David pivoted on his good leg and went back inside to answer it.

"David?"

Relief washed over him when he heard Marina's voice. "Damn it, where are you?" he demanded. "Are you all right?"

"I'm fine. I'm sorry if I worried you. I decided to go for a walk."

It was what Locatelli had suggested. David breathed deeply a few times before he spoke again. "Stefan was asking where you went."

"Is he all right?"

"Yes." He looked at the love seat in the living room. Stefan was curled into one corner as he watched a cartoon video on the wide-screen TV, his eyelids drooping. "He's practically asleep. I was just about to put him to bed."

"I want to see him," she said.

"Is that Miss Artomova?" Locatelli asked, stepping through the balcony doorway. "I'd like to speak with her."

David heard a muffled grunt from the phone. Marina spoke quickly. "No," she said. "David, I don't want to talk to him. I only want to talk to you. You're Stefan's father."

He frowned and held up his hand to stop Locatelli. "That's right."

"You're Stefan's legal father," she said, her tone carefully neutral. "We both know that."

"We can talk about this when you get back."

"No, there are policemen in my stateroom. I want to talk about this in private."

The relief David had felt when he'd answered the phone

began to ebb. This sounded off. She was speaking the way she did when they were arguing in front of Stefan and she didn't want him to understand her feelings through her tone. "What did you have in mind?" he asked.

"I want to talk to you on the Helios deck. Only you, me and Stefan. We're away from port, the ship is safe. There isn't any need to bring those guards."

"Marina…"

"I'll be waiting outside the children's center where we met before."

"You mean right now?"

"Yes. It's a lovely evening. He's been cooped up and the air will do him good."

"Marina—"

"I don't want to argue, David. You were right about everything."

"What?"

"I was only going through the motions. You can keep him. You're his father. Just let me see him tonight."

"Fine, Marina. We'll be right there."

"Thank you, David. I knew you'd understand."

The connection terminated. David dropped the phone and grabbed his crutches. She'd said the words he'd wanted to hear a week ago.

But it wasn't cause for celebration. Fear shot through his body, tightening his muscles and drying his throat. It was a bone-deep cold unlike anything he'd known before.

He'd been wrong. Waiting for Fedorovich to show up in the States wasn't the worst-case scenario. *This* was. He swung himself in front of Locatelli. "Fedorovich is here," he said. "He's got Marina."

"Is that what she said?"

"No, not specifically, but she gave me a message loud and clear."

"What exactly did Miss Artamova tell you?"

"She asked me to bring Stefan to meet her. Fedorovich was listening—you told me he speaks English. He must be forcing her to do this."

Locatelli exchanged a glance with Gallo, who had followed him through the door. It was almost identical to the expression on Gideon's face when David had told him about Stefan's monster. It was the same expression the guards had given Marina the night before when she'd demanded they search the veranda.

David felt his temper snap. Only the fact that Stefan was within earshot kept him from venting his frustration at the volume he wanted to use. He anchored one hand in Locatelli's sport coat and leaned over. "Call Gideon. Have him send everyone he's got to the Helios deck."

"Mr. Anderson," he said, his tone carefully patient. "The Russian police said Fedorovich is in Moscow."

David knew he didn't have a shred of evidence to back up his fear. He was going on nothing but instinct and gut feeling. Yet not for one heartbeat did he feel any doubt. "I don't give a damn what any of you say. Marina's in trouble. Fedorovich is using her to get to Stefan."

"I realize you've been under tremendous strain, Mr. Anderson, but—"

"Listen to me. I know this woman. She just told me she's dropping her custody suit, but she loves her nephew more than anything in her life. She would send him away with me if she thought it would keep him safe, but she would never voluntarily give him up. She *knows* that I know that. That's how I'm certain something's wrong."

The words were out before he could think about them. They had come so easily, he must have realized the truth all along.

He'd been deluding himself to think he could win. Whether he tried for ten days on a cruise ship or ten years in a courtroom, he would never convince Marina to let Stefan go.

And this was a hell of a time to figure that out.

THE BREEZE THAT HAD come up at sunset had stiffened as the evening had worn on, bringing the scent of salt water and the distinctive back-of-the-throat seaweed and fish tang of a distant shore. The lights of Palermo were lost behind them as the dark bulk of Sicily slid past along the horizon. If Marina closed her eyes, she could almost pretend she was a child again, back on her father's fishing boat. Although the air was warmer, and the swells that the ship rode through were no more than a suggestion of motion, the smell of the sea was similar enough to give her a moment of peace.

Fedorovich wedged the muzzle of his gun into the underside of her breast. The silencer on the end of the barrel poked hard through the silk and lace that covered her flesh. "It has been more than thirty minutes," he muttered in Russian.

Tears of pain blurred her vision. She blinked them away and focused on the deck. "Please, don't kill me. Give them a few more minutes. You heard him agree."

He shifted his grip on her arm, positioning her more squarely on the bench beside him, then leaned over to spit at her feet.

Marina gagged as a drop of the warm spittle splashed

on her ankle, but she made no move to free herself from his grasp. She had to make Fedorovich believe she was a coward, that she was so terrified of him that she would do whatever he said, including talking David into bringing her nephew to meet her. Stefan's life depended on her ability to control herself.

So she swallowed hard instead of twisting around to spit in his face the way she longed to. She curled her nails into her palms instead of driving them into his eyes. She acted subdued and beaten. She controlled the urge she felt to bite and claw and kick....

It was the hardest thing she'd ever done.

But this was for Stefan. She needed to restrain her emotions. She had to act logically. She tried to think the way David would.

He must have understood her. Oh, please God, let him have realized she hadn't meant what she'd said. It had been the best she could manage with Fedorovich listening to every word of their conversation, but David was a smart man. He could put two and two together and realize she'd been warning him.

She glanced around, but she could see no sign of any Italian police or the ship's security force. Fedorovich had said they would have canceled their alert and withdrawn their people because they would be looking for him in Moscow instead of here. But they had to be out there, she reassured herself. They were just getting into position, that's all. She had to keep Fedorovich here until they were ready to move in. It could be their only opportunity to stop him.

Yet it wouldn't be easy for anyone to sneak up on them. Fedorovich had chosen this spot well. They were on the topmost deck, the most open location on the ship. Although the putting green was empty and no one had appeared on the tennis courts for a while, the deck wasn't deserted. Every now and then the breeze brought snatches of conversation from the people who strolled along the railing, or music from the outdoor movie theater. But no one wandered near the shadows where Fedorovich had brought her.

They were sitting on the same bench where Marina had sat with David last week as they'd watched Stefan play. The children's center was dark now. Only the reflection of the stars showed in the glass. The wooden planters that decorated the area helped hide them from view. To anyone passing by, they would appear to be a couple out to enjoy the stars in privacy.

But Fedorovich wasn't looking at the sky, he was watching the access points to the deck. He was sitting so close to Marina, she could feel the tremors of excitement that went through him whenever someone arrived on the deck with a child. Thankfully, no one had arrived recently. Because each time a child had appeared, she had felt Fedorovich's finger move against her breast.

She knew he wasn't stroking her, he was stroking the barrel of his gun.

It made her sick.

"Why can't you just let us go?" she asked. The tremor in her voice scared her—it wasn't feigned.

"Because I'm a man of honor." He leaned over to spit again. "That's something you would not understand."

Dark streaks mixed with the spittle. It looked like blood. She fought a wave of nausea. "You killed my sister."

"Yes, she died quickly. Her neck snapped when the car rolled over. There was little blood on her. There was much more on the man. The steering column cleaved his chest in two."

Oh, God, he was stroking his gun again. Marina tried to shut out his words as he went on to describe the details of the accident he'd caused. His tone was without inflection, as if he made no distinction between the wreckage of Borya's car and the shattered lives of human beings.

"The boy was meant to die nine months ago," he continued. "I am merely the instrument of his death."

"How much were you paid?" she asked quickly. "I can double it if you spare him."

His finger stilled. "You are nothing but a *novye russkie*. Your kind ruined our country, pursuing wealth over honor like any capitalist."

"What honor is there in killing an innocent child? There would be more honor in mercy."

"Mercy?" He took his hand from her arm and grabbed her hair. "This is what mercy brings," he said, wrenching her head around so that her face was inches from his cheek.

A dark beard covered the lower half of his face. That was why she hadn't recognized him immediately when he'd caught her beside the elevator. He hadn't been able to hide his shovel-blade nose or his deep-set eyes, but by the time she'd noticed them, she'd felt his gun against her ribs.

He hadn't threatened to shoot Marina to make her cooperate. Instead he'd threatened to shoot the woman and infant who had been waiting for the elevator beside her.

The terror she'd felt when she'd gone with him hadn't been feigned, either.

She focused on the edge of what had to be a fake beard. It couldn't completely cover Fedorovich's distinctive scar. A thick, white line, visible even in the shadows, curved from beneath the beard to the outer edge of his cheekbone.

"The boy I spared was no older than the Gorsky boy,"

he said. "He was herding goats near his village and saw my patrol. I let him go because I was a weak fool. He brought back soldiers who cut my men to pieces and left me with this." He shoved her forehead into his cheek, then returned his grip to her arm and dragged her upright once more. "I did not make that mistake a second time."

She didn't want to hear this, but the longer she could keep him talking and keep him here, the better chance there was that help would come. Locatelli had said Fedorovich had fought in Afghanistan. That must be what he was describing. "It was war. This isn't."

"The lessons are the same. When I returned to that village, I spared no one. Not the boy or his little sisters or the old women who screamed in the corners. I left nothing alive in that valley, not even the goats." He sat taller beside her, as if proud of the atrocity he was relating. "Afterward, I was made a colonel."

He was truly insane, she realized. A psychopath. The army should have given him psychiatric treatment instead of a promotion. There would be no reasoning with this man, no possibility of appealing to his conscience. If he wasn't stopped now, Stefan would never be safe.

"I have waited nine months to finish my duty." His voice was getting thick, as if he were gathering saliva and blood in his mouth again. "It will be all the sweeter when I do."

"Is that why you waited?"

"The boy disappeared. I tracked him to the orphanage but I could not locate him. Then you did it for me."

"What?"

"I have many eyes and ears who watched you search for your nephew. I learned when you found him and I followed you to this ship."

It took her a moment to understand what he'd said. Fedorovich had followed her. She had led him to *Alexandra's Dream*. She had led him to Stefan.

Oh, God. Of all the horrors he'd related so far, this was the one that cut her the deepest. It was because of *her* that this monster was here. Her love for her nephew had put him in danger.

"You brought me to him. It is fitting that you now bring him to me. *There.*"

Marina whipped her head toward the direction Fedorovich was looking. A tall, dark-haired man had moved into the pool of light on the far side of the tennis courts and paused on the deck as if getting his bearings.

Panic bubbled through her chest. No! David wasn't supposed to come. He was supposed to send the security men. Hadn't he understood?

"I don't see the boy," Fedorovich snarled.

All right. David *had* understood, Marina realized. He had both hands on his crutches. He didn't have Stefan with him. Thank God, her nephew was safe....

Her heart slammed into a wall of ice. If David had understood her message, then why had he come at all? He should have stayed with Stefan and let the experts deal with Fedorovich. That's why she'd gone along with the madman's demands. That's why she'd been pretending docility, so no one else would have to get hurt.

But now David was here. She'd put him in danger, too. And Fedorovich was moving his gun away from her breast and—

"No!" she screamed, jerking away from his hold. "David, go back!"

Her voice echoed across the deck into a sudden silence.

When had the music from the movie theater stopped? She could see no one strolling along the deck or standing near the railing, either. There was only David, spotlighted against the night sky as he balanced on his crutches. He was alone and unarmed, and would be an easy target for a trained soldier and an assassin.

Fedorovich locked his arm around Marina's throat. Holding her in front of him, he rose from the bench. "Where's the boy?" he called in English.

Instead of retreating, David planted the tips of his crutches on the deck and moved forward. "He's safe. You will never hurt him."

"Have him brought to me or I will kill her."

Marina winced as she felt the muzzle of the gun press into the hollow behind her earlobe. "Go ahead," she said. "You were supposed to kill the Gorsky family. I'm Borya's sister-in-law. Kill me instead of Stefan."

David's crutches thumped faster on the deck as he increased his speed. "Marina, shut up!"

"Stay where you are, Anderson," Fedorovich ordered. He dragged Marina backward until they came up against the glass wall of the children's center.

"Yes, kill me instead," Marina repeated. "That should satisfy your honor. Then this can end."

"Marina, be quiet. You don't need to do this," David shouted. He had reached the first of the wooden planter boxes and had to slow down to maneuver around it. "Fedorovich is a coward. He has no honor. He's shielding himself behind a woman."

Fedorovich jerked as if he'd been struck. The pressure of the gun muzzle lessened. "You know nothing. You are an American. Soft and weak."

"I don't hide behind women," David said. "Or threaten cripples. You're a coward."

Even through her panic Marina was aware that David was deliberately taunting Fedorovich to draw his attention away from her. What was wrong with the man? Didn't he realize his only priority should be protecting Stefan? "David, don't worry about me!" she cried. "Get out of here! Get help!"

"No honor," David said. He didn't need to shout any longer. He was almost at the end of the bench where they'd been sitting. "Look at him. He's a disgrace to any uniform."

Fedorovich spat on the deck. "Fool! You court a hero's death, but that will not save the boy." He took the gun from Marina's neck and pointed it at David. "I do not need you to bring him to me. I will find him again after I kill you both. I never fail."

"No!" Marina burst into motion. She kicked backward and clawed at Fedorovich's arm just as he pulled the trigger. Something whizzed past her ear, tugging at her hair.

Fedorovich shoved Marina aside and straightened his arm to point his gun directly at David's chest.

"Marina, run!" David yelled. *"Get out of here!"*

She had no intention of obeying him. She lunged for Fedorovich, wanting to knock him off balance, spoil his aim, anything, before he could pull the trigger, but her feet slid on the pool of spittle he'd left on the deck. She fell to her knees, her palms smacking hard on the wood, yet she managed to tip her shoulder into Fedorovich's leg. The bullet thudded into the back of the bench.

Light flooded the area. From the corner of her vision, Marina saw uniformed men jog toward them on all sides.

"Drop your gun, Fedorovich!" It was Locatelli's voice,

amplified by a megaphone. It was accompanied by the metallic clicking of weapons being readied. "We have you surrounded."

Marina lifted her head and saw Fedorovich move his gaze over the deck. His dark eyes gleamed, as if the sight of the armed men excited him.

"Put down the weapon," Locatelli ordered. "There is no way out."

Beneath the dark beard, Fedorovich's jaw moved as if he were chewing something. He straightened his spine as proudly as he had when he'd spoken of his murderous rampage in the war. "First, I will complete my duty," he said in Russian, tipping his weapon away from David.

"That's it," Locatelli said. "Now toss the gun away and put your hands on your head."

They hadn't understood what he'd said, Marina realized, sliding farther away from Fedorovich. "He's not surrendering," she shouted.

Fedorovich's teeth gleamed as he swung the gun at Marina. "You were right. You are part of the fisherman's family. Your death will serve—"

"No!" David tossed one crutch aside, grasped the other with both hands and swung it at Fedorovich. The tip struck him above the ear with enough force to crunch bone, knocking him off his feet and sending him head-first into the steel support of the bench.

But not before the hit man's gun discharged again. David fell backward to the deck.

"Move in, move in!" Locatelli ordered.

Time shifted to the slow-motion pace of a nightmare. Marina was dimly aware of the noise of booted feet. She could hear both Locatelli and Gideon issuing orders as men brushed past her to reach Fedorovich. Radios crackled, more people arrived on the deck, but all she could see, all she could think about, was how motionless David was.

She crawled across the deck to his side. His eyes were open, his chest was rising and falling, but his breathing sounded strained. There was a round hole in the center of his golf shirt....

Oh, *no!* She placed her palm on David's chest. "Get a doctor!" she cried to the people around her.

David lifted his hand to stroke her cheek. "Marina," he rasped. "I'm okay."

She turned her head to kiss his fingers. "Save your strength, Davochik," she whispered.

"Marina, I'm fine. Really."

"Mr. Anderson?" It was the ship's captain, Nikolas Pappas. He squatted beside David and peered into his face. "Are you hurt?"

"Just winded," David replied. "That's all. I don't need a doctor."

The captain tossed out a command to one of the other officers who was tending to Fedorovich, then squeezed David's shoulder, straightened and moved off.

Marina stared at Captain Pappas in disbelief. Couldn't he see? She took David's hand between both of hers, her tears falling on his knuckles. "You ridiculous, maddening man. This isn't the time to be brave. You need—"

"Marina, look at me." He clenched his jaw and pushed up on one elbow. "I'm wearing a vest."

She looked at his chest again. There was no blood around the bullet hole. She could see no skin beneath the fabric. And now that she was starting to breathe again, she noticed his chest looked bulkier than it should have. That's when she realized that beneath his beige golf shirt, David was wearing a bulletproof vest.

The relief was so intense, it was painful. The tears flowed faster, welling from her eyes to drip all over his wonderful, baggy, boring clothes. David was unhurt. He really was fine. She wasn't going to lose another person she loved.

Marina's lungs heaved. She doubled over, hugging David's hand to her breasts.

"Hey, are you all right?" David asked.

Another person she loved. Not just liked, not only on-the-verge of falling, but completely over-the-edge in love. She loved David. She didn't want to lose him. She felt his presence in her heart as surely as she felt his hand in hers.

"Marina?"

But she was going to lose him. They'd been fated to part from the beginning. Her shoulders began to tremble. She sat back on her heels and snatched her hands from his.

Time once again slipped back into its track. Officer Gallo and one of Gideon's men dragged Fedorovich away. He didn't look like a monster now. He was completely limp. His head lolled between his shoulders. Blood ran down his temple from the place where David had struck him.

David sat up and took her chin in his hand. He turned her head, looking at one side and then the other. "Did that first shot hit you? I thought he missed."

She gulped for air. The concern in his voice was making it hard for her to breathe again. She looked at the deck, at the railing, at the stars in the sky, anywhere except into the face that had become so dear to her.

She loved him. Oh, *God!* She hadn't wanted this to happen. "I'm fine. Where's Stefan?" she asked. "Who's watching him? He could be worried. I need to see him."

"Stefan can wait," David said, shifting his hands to her cheeks. "This can't."

"What—"

He stopped her words with a kiss.

By this time, Marina was trembling so badly, she didn't notice that David was, too.

CHAPTER THIRTEEN

THE SEA WAS restless, its long swells puckered with rows of marching waves. The breeze hadn't died during the night, and it was strengthening with the sunrise. To the east, the sky was already tinted with pink, laying a glistening path on the water for *Alexandra's Dream* to follow. David was in no hurry to see the dawn. It meant they had only one day left. He turned away from the window and focused on the bed.

Marina was sitting on the edge of the mattress, her hand on Stefan's shoulder. She'd been desperate to get back to her stateroom to see him. That was the only thing she'd wanted to talk about throughout the interview with Locatelli. She'd had no patience for their questions or for the words of praise the ship's staff and the Italian police had tried to give her. She'd flat-out refused to be examined by a doctor. All she'd wanted was to come back and hug her nephew.

David had found it hard to let go of her, even for Stefan. He was too conscious of the time that was slipping away.

At first the night had seemed endless. The forty minutes between Marina's phone call and Locatelli's signal had been an eternity. David had wanted the police to move in immediately, but Captain Pappas had refused to permit them to storm the deck until it could be sealed off and the passengers who were already there could be removed to safety. Although David had understood his concern, and the security chief had accomplished the evacuation as quickly and quietly as possible, every second they had delayed had been too long.

Yet when he had seen Fedorovich's gun point at Marina, time had collapsed altogether.

David rubbed his eyes, trying to erase the image in his head. She was safe, he reminded himself. She was unharmed. So was Stefan.

Fedorovich was handcuffed to a bed in the ship's medical center. He would remain under guard until Locatelli took him off the ship, but he hadn't yet regained consciousness. There was a chance he never would. According to the ship's doctor, David's blow had fractured his skull and driven pieces of bone into his brain.

He knew he should be sorry, but he wasn't. Maybe someday, when the memory of that nightmare-come-to-life had faded, he would find some sympathy for Ilya Fedorovich. Maybe. It wouldn't happen anytime soon.

Until now, David had never raised his hand against another human being. He was fully aware of his size, and the power in his muscles. He'd inherited his physique from his biological father, and he used it to his advantage in every sport he played. Yet not once had he resorted to violence, no matter what the provocation.

He'd been as careful to control his strength as he had been to control his emotions. He knew how destructive both could be. He'd borne the consequences of his birth mother's impulsiveness. His very conception had been a mistake. And his back was a constant reminder of what happened when a man's strength was perverted to cruelty.

Because of that, he'd always lived his life with his passions in check. It had been one of the factors that had led to his divorce. Ellie hadn't realized that simply because he wasn't showy about his feelings didn't mean he was incapable of them.

Yet that hadn't deterred Marina. All it took was one touch, one look from her, even just a thought of her, and there was no way to shove his emotions back inside.

She'd done something to him. He hadn't seen it coming, because he'd been preoccupied with her effect on Stefan, not himself. He hadn't needed to shield his feelings around Stefan. He'd opened his heart to the boy…and Marina had slipped inside along with him.

He glanced at the sky again, then pushed away from the window and went to the bed. "Marina?" he whispered.

She turned to look at him. In the light from the bathroom doorway, he could see that her cheeks were wet.

He took her hand from Stefan's shoulder and tugged her to her feet. "He's asleep."

"He looks like an angel."

David stroked her hair. "He's safe now, Marina. Please, stop crying."

She wiped her cheeks with the backs of her hands. "This is my fault. I brought that maniac here."

David slipped his arm around her shoulders, tucked a crutch under his other arm and steered her out of the bedroom. Anyone would be upset after what Marina had gone through, yet it was more than being held hostage at gunpoint that was causing her distress.

She'd told the police everything that Fedorovich had

said, including how he'd followed her to Stefan. The latest update from Interpol had supported Fedorovich's claim— the Moscow informant who had given the Russian authorities a false tip had turned out to be the doorman of Marina's apartment building. He had served in the army with Fedorovich and had admitted reporting Marina's whereabouts to him.

"You couldn't have known," David said, closing the door behind them. "No one did."

She eased away from him and walked to the living room. It was blazing with lights, as it had been when the last of the guards had left. She moved around to switch them off, then paused beside the coffee table to pick up one of Stefan's picture books. "I never wanted to hurt him," she said. "I only wanted to love him."

"And you do, Marina. Anyone can see that."

"But I put him in danger. I've made him cry." She tipped the book toward the lamp she'd left on and ran her fingertips over the smiling tugboat on the cover. "You don't do that. You give him games to play and books to read. You always seem to know exactly what he needs."

"Marina…"

"You believed him. You wanted to fight his monster but I'm the one who led the monster here."

"Fedorovich won't hurt anyone again, Marina. It's over. You've got to stop blaming yourself."

She tossed the book onto the love seat. Her gaze fell on the lopsided boat that he and Stefan had made from building blocks. She bent to pick it up and held it to her chest. Her lips trembled.

"It's more than Fedorovich, isn't it?" David asked gently. "What's wrong, Marina?"

"I'm afraid, David. What if Olena was right?"

"About what?"

"I'm not meant to be a mother. I've been fooling myself to believe that I could make a good parent."

"That's not true."

"Isn't it? You've spent the past nine days pointing out what a terrible mother I would be."

"I was critical of you because I wanted to win."

"But you were right, too. I don't follow schedules, I don't care about vitamins or food groups, and I never discipline."

"Sure, but you're creative, you're honest and you have incredible insights."

"You've got a family. Brothers and sisters and parents who can give Stefan a kind of security I never could."

"You speak his language. You understand where he comes from."

"You've got a room ready for him. You probably have boxes of toys and closets full of clothes." She put the building-block boat on top of the book and glanced around the suite. "I've got a luxury apartment with a million breakables."

"Knowing you, you'd make a game of throwing them all into your fireplace. Right after you let him throw food around your bathtub."

"You know how to take care of him."

"You know how to make him laugh," he said. It didn't strike him as odd that they were arguing each other's cases. Lately, the battle lines had become as blurred as his emotions. "And I am absolutely certain that whatever off-the-wall impulse you might decide to follow, you would never pin a note to his chest and abandon him in a diner."

She inhaled sharply and looked at him. He could tell by the softening at the corners of her eyes that she understood he was talking about his own mother. "No, I would never do that," she said.

She would never betray someone she loved, either, he thought, the way his ex-wife had betrayed him. He might have known Marina for only nine days, but he understood that, for her, love was forever. "So the fact that Fedorovich followed you doesn't mean anything. You couldn't have given up your search for Stefan. You had to find him. It wouldn't have been possible for you to do things differently. That's just the kind of woman you are."

Some of the distress eased from her gaze. She sat on one arm of the sofa. "I still feel guilty."

"That's because you feel everything. You don't hold back." He moved closer. "Your sister was wrong about you, Marina. You can give a child what matters the most."

"What?"

"Love."

"Don't patronize me, David."

"I'm not." He leaned his crutch against an armchair and covered the rest of the distance without it. "You once told me that I should never question your love."

She wiped her forearm across her eyes. "Yes, I remember. I said that the day we met."

"You should take your own advice, Marina. You've spent too many years trying to convince yourself that you won't find love. Now you're doubting your own."

"David…"

"You're an exceptional woman. You would make a wonderful parent. You have more courage than anyone I've known."

"How can you say that?" She flung out her arms. "I'm not brave. Look at me. I'm a wreck. I wasn't able to stop crying long enough to kiss my nephew good-night because my tears would wake him up."

"That's my point. It takes courage to love someone. The strength of your love for your nephew humbles me. You risked your life for him."

"This isn't helping," she muttered, blinking back another wave of tears.

He reached out to dry her cheeks with his thumb. "You risked your life for me, too."

She looked away. "I don't want to talk about this anymore, David."

"Well, I do. You didn't run when you had the chance. You tried to knock off Fedorovich's aim."

"I didn't know you were wearing a bulletproof vest."

He took her hand. "You cried when you thought I was shot."

"Because that would have been my fault, too. I only wanted you to warn Locatelli when I phoned you. I hadn't wanted you to come. I was counting on you to be sensible."

"Sensible wasn't an option. I thought I'd go crazy when I found out Fedorovich had you." He squeezed her fingers. "I wanted to throttle you myself when I heard you try to talk him into taking your life instead of Stefan's."

"I had to do something."

"It was reckless."

"It would have solved our custody dispute."

He yanked her off the sofa arm. He'd said the same words to her last week. He hadn't realized then how much they would hurt. "Don't say that. Don't even think it."

She fisted her hands on his chest. "Why not? We can't pretend it's not between us."

He pressed his cheek to the side of her head. "Try."

"Our truce is over. Fedorovich is caught. There's no reason for you to stay in my suite anymore. When Stefan wakes up, you'll take him away again."

"This isn't about Stefan." He rubbed his nose over her hair. "David—"

"Just let me hold you, okay?"

She shuddered. "Do you think I'm an idiot? I know you want more than that."

"Marina…"

"You want to finish what we started yesterday."

He found the rim of her ear and nudged her hair aside so he could nuzzle it. "Yes. Don't you?"

She thumped his shoulder. "That would be stupid."

"Why?"

"You're a wreck, too. I know you're exhausted. I can see you're in pain because you've got circles under your eyes and those lines beside your mouth are tight but instead of taking care of yourself you're trying to make me feel better." She tipped her head to meet his gaze. "And then you limp across the room to hold me and I see that bullet hole still in your shirt and I keep thinking about how you could have been shot."

He grasped his shirt, yanked it over his head and tossed it behind him. "There. Is that better?"

Her eyes darkened. "Damn you, David. I don't *want* to want this."

"Neither do I. It doesn't stop how I feel."

She opened her fists to hold her palms a whisper from his skin. "It's almost dawn."

"Not yet." He reached out to turn off the lamp, then caught her hands, lifted them to his mouth and kissed them. From there, he moved to her wrists, kissing the undersides where he could feel her pulse beating. The sleeves of her dress were loose enough to slide back, so he kissed his way along her arm until he could dip his tongue against the warm fold of skin on the inside of her elbow.

Moaning, she swayed into him and locked her arms behind his neck, pressing her body full-length to his. For long, trembling minutes they simply stood there in silence, warming each other, holding each other, allowing their senses to absorb the connection. David felt his breathing steady as it meshed with hers, their chests rising and falling in unison. Once again, they were simply David and Marina, two people thrown together by fate, neither wanting to let go. And gradually, inevitably, the embrace began to change.

The motions were subtle. She shifted her shoulders while he tightened his arms. Her breasts molded to his chest more firmly as they swelled. When he moved his hips to ease the pressure that was beginning to build, she slid her hand between them and cupped him through his pants.

David shook from the force of the arousal that crashed over him. He knew some of it had to be an aftereffect of adrenaline. It was a well-known fact that danger got the blood pumping. There was no question he and Marina shared a powerful physical chemistry, too, a natural consequence of two healthy adults living in close proximity.

But what he felt was more than physical. He'd understood that for days. He didn't want to have sex with Marina. He wanted to make love.

Cradling her face in his hands, David finally brought his mouth to hers. There was no longer any need for preliminaries. Marina parted her lips for him as soon as he touched them. The kiss was different from the ones they'd shared before. Deeper. More certain...and more urgent.

Marina reached for his belt buckle at the same moment

he hiked up her dress to her hips. While she lowered his zipper, he slipped his hand between her thighs. She was as honest with her passion as everything else, responding eagerly to each caress he gave her with two of her own. There was no room for hesitancy or shyness. They shoved aside clothing, not waiting to take it off, too impatient to complete what their kiss was promising. The lack of a bed didn't stop them. Nor did his sprained knee. With Marina's legs hooked around his waist, he lowered her to the sofa.

Her teeth closed around his tongue as he entered her. David thrust deeper and felt her nails dig into his back. The scent of apples and sex rose from her skin, as intimate as the sounds of their bodies joining. It was raw, hard and primal, and exactly what they both needed.

At least, that's what he thought. Until he kissed her cheek and tasted the salt of fresh tears.

He lifted his head. "Marina, are you all right? I'm sorry, was I too rough?"

She hiccuped and fisted her hand in his hair to bring his face back to hers. "No, I'm fine. It was wonderful."

"Then why—" He licked a tear that trickled from the corner of her eye. "Why are you crying again?"

"Because it would be truly ridiculous to fall in love with my enemy."

He dropped his face to the crook of her neck. His body, still throbbing from the force of their climax, shuddered with a completion that had nothing to do with sex. He gasped, trying to catch his breath.

She slid her hand down his back and dragged her nails along his buttocks. "I tried not to, but I couldn't help it. I do love you, David."

"Marina—"

"But don't think it's because you have Stefan. I wouldn't say that just because I want my nephew. I do, but that isn't why I love you. And it's not because I'm grateful you risked your life for me."

He shook his head and nipped her earlobe.

"Don't think I'm giving up, either. I just—"

He clamped his arm around her back, dragged her to the carpet and rolled her on top of him. He grasped her face in his hands. "Marina, are you going to make an argument out of this, too?"

"David…"

"I think I fell in love with you the first time you bared your teeth at me, but I wouldn't let myself see it. You're fierce and impulsive, and you're perfect for me. I had no choice. You made me love you."

"Me? You're the one who's **so** sensitive and sweet." She tweaked a curl of his chest hair. "You deliberately seduced me."

"You make me crazy."

She smiled. "And you, my darling Davochik, make me feel like anything's possible."

MARINA AWOKE TO THE sound of clinking cutlery and whispered laughter. She blinked and looked around, disoriented for a moment until she realized it was full daylight and she was still in the living room. It had already been getting light when she and David had opened the sofa into a bed. Of course, it had been another incredible hour before they'd finally fallen asleep.

"I think she's awake," David murmured. "Go ahead."

Marina pushed herself up on her elbows and looked toward the dining room.

David was standing in front of a room service cart that was loaded with covered platters. He was wearing one of the white velour robes that had come with the stateroom, his hair wet and his cheeks gleaming from a fresh shave. Stefan, still wearing his pajamas, had both hands clutched around a bud vase that held a single red rose. He glanced at David, who nodded, then carried the flower to Marina.

She clutched the blanket to her chest with one hand and reached for the vase with the other. "Thank you, Stefan."

He grinned, bounced onto the bed, and started speaking in Russian. His blue eyes, so much like his mother's, were sparkling with a light she hadn't seen since his birthday party the year before.

David followed more slowly. He wasn't using his crutch this morning, and his limp wasn't as pronounced as the day before. A lock of wet hair covered the healing scrape on his forehead and the one on his cheek was nearly gone, yet he still had the look of a wounded warrior.

A smiling, sexually satisfied one.

A wave of tenderness tightened her throat, making it hard to speak. Oh, how she loved this man. She would have loved him even if they'd never touched, but sleeping with him had only driven him deeper into her heart. She lifted her face as he leaned down to kiss her. Tingles shot through her body, warming places that still ached from their lovemaking.

He stroked her hair from her cheek with his knuckle, his gaze alight with a promise of more to come, before he looked past her to Stefan. "What's he saying?" he asked.

She brought the flower to her nose and drew in the scent as she looked at her nephew.

He had crawled under the blanket and was snuggled into

the pillow that David had used. It reminded her of the way she and Olena used to climb into their parents' bed when they'd been children. How innocent those times had seemed, and how simple. She hadn't yet known change, or loss. Tucked between her mother and father, surrounded by the sheets their bodies had warmed, she'd been safe and loved and *home*.

Her eyes heated. Home. It wasn't a place, it was a feeling. That's why she'd been able to carry it with her all those years.

David sat beside her on the mattress and ran his fingertip down her arm. "Marina?"

"He's talking about naps."

"He doesn't look tired."

"No, not his naps. He said when his father came home from a fishing trip, he and Olena had lots of naps in their room, and after they got up, his mother would sing while she cooked and his father would always be in a good mood—" She bit her lip, realization dawning on exactly what her sister and brother-in-law must have been doing.

"My son is a smart boy," David said. He ruffled Stefan's hair and pointed to the dining room. "Can you bring Aunt Nina breakfast?"

Stefan wriggled out from beneath the blanket and scrambled over the back of the sofa to drop to the floor. He went to the room service cart and started lifting the covers from the platters.

"It's good to hear him talk about his parents," David said quietly. "He must be feeling more secure."

Stefan poked his finger into a pastry and withdrew what appeared to be strawberry filling. He licked it off and dug in for more.

Odd that David had ordered pastries instead of something wholesome and nutritious, Marina thought. "He's acting more like the child I remember," she said. "I wonder if he senses that his nightmare is over."

"That's possible. He's very sensitive to moods." David rose from the sofa bed to retrieve a second velour robe like his that was folded over the back of a chair. He draped it around Marina's shoulders. "Stefan might be too young to realize why you woke up smiling," he said, kissing her ear. "But he recognizes love when he sees it."

That was probably the main reason for Stefan's buoyant mood, Marina thought, slipping her arms into the sleeves of the robe. Love meant home to him, too. "David…"

He pressed his thumb to her lower lip. "I need to talk to you about Stefan, Marina, but I don't want you to get the wrong idea, so hear me out before you start arguing, okay?"

"All right."

"I know you're not going to give up," he said. "I'm not going to give up, either, but I can't afford to fight you in court, so I have a solution."

She had one, too. It seemed obvious to her now, but she should let David have his say. He was a methodical, rational man and it might take some time to convince him. It wouldn't be easy for him to trust a woman who said she loved him, so she should think it through before she ambushed him. He hadn't taken well to that before, and he could be stubborn at times.

The phone began to ring. David gave it a look of exasperation.

Marina fastened the belt of her robe and flipped the blanket off her legs. "I'd better answer that."

"They'll call back."

"What if it's Locatelli?"

David sighed and went to answer the phone just as Stefan returned with a plate full of pastries. Most of them had finger-size holes in the top. Marina held on to the plate as Stefan climbed back on the bed and started on the largest Danish. A blob of strawberry jelly oozed down his chin to fall on the blanket.

Marina scooped the jelly onto her finger and popped it in her mouth as she watched David.

His expression had closed up. He held out the phone to her. "It's your lawyer."

She set the plate on the bed and went to take the phone from David. She didn't like the interruption, but she was glad that Rudolph had called. She would need to talk to him later anyway.

"Marina, I have good news!" he said as soon as she'd said hello. "We've won."

"What?"

"It's over. Your nephew will not be going to America."

It took a second for his words to sink in. These were the words she'd wanted to hear for weeks. It was why she'd booked her ticket, it was her reason for being on the ship, for knowing David, for everything that she'd done. She rubbed her palm over her robe and switched the phone to her other hand. "Rudolph, are you sure?"

"Positive."

They were speaking in Russian, so she knew that David wouldn't be able to understand the conversation, but Stefan could. She carried the phone to the dining room and sat at the table. "How?" she asked, keeping her voice low. "Were the travel documents revoked?"

"No, it's better than that. The adoption was based on fraud. It's going to be canceled."

"Fraud? You mean, David did something wrong?"

He must have heard his name. He crossed his arms and looked at her. She tried to give him a reassuring smile but her cheeks felt frozen.

"No, it was the admissions clerk at the Murmansk orphanage. She finally came forward this morning because of the police investigation that Mr. Anderson instigated. She admitted that she changed Stefan Gorsky's name and misplaced his file when she transferred him to the orphanage in St. Petersburg."

"Why?"

"She did it to protect your nephew. She'd heard rumors that someone from the *Mafiya* was looking for him last summer after the accident, so she made him disappear. It wasn't a clerical error, it was deliberate tampering."

Marina rubbed her forehead. It was hard to take in, yet it made sense. *This* was why there had been no traces to follow, and why all the records had been so thoroughly lost. Rudolph had told her she was being dramatic when she'd claimed there had been a conspiracy at the orphanage to keep her from Stefan, but she'd been right. Not about the reason, though. She'd thought it had been done for profit, but it had been done to save Stefan's life.

"Marina, if not for the clerk's actions, the adoption would not have taken place. It is illegal. No court will uphold it."

She looked at Stefan. He was sitting cross-legged in front of the pastry plate, strawberry jelly smeared up both of his cheeks like a grin. "What's going to happen to the clerk? She's not going to get into trouble, is she?"

"It's possible she'll lose her job."

"Bribe someone to make sure that she doesn't. Or if

you can't prevent it, we'll offer her a position at the Moscow store."

"I'll look into it if you insist."

"I do. She saved his life."

His sigh crackled through the receiver. "Marina, I believe you're missing the point. If we could return to the matter I called you about…"

"Where would Stefan go if the adoption were canceled?"

"He would have to return to the orphanage, but that would only be a temporary placement. We would petition for guardianship immediately."

"That's not good enough," she said. "I won't send Stefan back to that place, even for an hour. Not after what he's gone through. He's only beginning to recover. He would never understand."

"Marina, it's the only avenue open to us if we wish to bring Stefan home. I'm obtaining an emergency injunction this afternoon. By tomorrow, both the travel papers and the adoption will be nullified."

"No."

"Excuse me?"

"I want you to stop what you're doing, Rudolph. Let the adoption stand."

"But—"

"Withdraw our protest, cancel the custody suit, forget the injunction. I want you to stop everything."

"Perhaps you don't understand. You've won."

"Not yet, Rudolph. But I intend to."

There was a silence. "Marina, I don't like the sound of that. What are you planning?"

The conversation was beginning to sound familiar. "I'll call you tomorrow with an update," she said. She terminated the connection to cut off the protest she knew was coming and placed the phone on the table.

Then she pressed the heels of her hands to her eyes, tipped back her head and swore silently in every language that she knew. She had either made the biggest mistake of her life, or…

"What was that about?" David asked.

She lowered her hands and looked at him. He was using a washcloth to clean Stefan's face but Stefan was already dipping his thumb into a cream puff. Strawberry jelly smeared the sleeve of David's robe. His belt had loosened, giving her a tantalizing glimpse of his chest and muscled abdomen.

The last of her doubts simply dissolved. Why on earth was she hesitating? Everything that she'd wanted, what she'd longed for in her heart but had never dared to seek, was right here in front of her. Someone to love her, and someone to love.

Marina knew she could trust David. It was trusting herself that needed work.

She smiled and walked over to kiss Stefan's forehead, then slid her arms around David's waist. "I love you, David Anderson. Will you marry me?"

He dropped the washcloth. So many emotions flashed through his gaze at once, she couldn't tell what he was feeling until he started to laugh.

She stomped on his toes. "Why are you laughing? I just proposed to you."

He moved his foot. "Marina, you couldn't wait, could you? I just spent the last half hour getting Stefan to teach me how to say that in Russian."

She glanced at her nephew. His eyes were lit with a conspirator's grin. Now she understood the real reason for his good mood. Leaving one arm around David, she held out her other hand to Stefan. He slipped off the mattress and joined their embrace.

Even though she knew they were on a ship, she could almost hear a train whistle in the background. It was that feeling again, the sense of coming home, of not being alone anymore. She'd been wrong to think she and David had been fated to part. Fate had brought all three of them together because surely this was meant to be.

She smiled at David. "Well, a proposal would sound much better in Russian, but now that I've asked, the least you could do is give me an answer."

"*Da*, Marina." He pulled her closer and spoke against her lips. "I'll marry you."

"We still need to decide where we'll live. I suppose it would be more logical for me to come to your home since Stefan would have a bigger family there. I could see about expanding my stores in America. Rudolph can help with that. And there are some technicalities with Stefan's adoption you'll need to straighten out. We should plan—"

As he'd done so often, David stopped her words with a kiss. He was still smiling when he lifted his head. "Marina," he said. "I love you, and you love me. That's enough for any relationship. We'll sort out the details later."

* * * * *

MEDITERRANEAN NIGHTS
Join the glamorous world of cruising with the guests
and crew of Alexandra's Dream—*the newest luxury ship*
to set sail on the romantic Mediterranean.
The voyage continues in July 2007 with
SCENT OF A WOMAN
by Joanne Rock.

Danielle Chevalier, a French perfumer,
sees the exclusive conference aboard Alexandra's Dream
as the perfect opportunity to make contacts necessary to
avoid a takeover of her fragrance business.
But when she meets Adam Burns, the competitor,
she realizes that not falling in love may be
her real battle....
Here's a preview!

"SO I GATHER I WOULD be able to sniff out individual ingredients in a woman's fragrance if I was a real perfumer, right?"

Danielle watched Adam settle into a deck chair beside her from their quiet corner on the observation deck that night. When she had arrived, he had already tugged the loungers into an isolated space and had a bottle of Riesling with two glasses ready on a small table between them. For her part, she was grateful to leave the perfume conference behind for the night.

She took her first sip of the wine while she thought about Adam's question.

"Perfume is like music, with layers of notes the discerning artist can pick out immediately in an elaborate composition. Because Les Rêves is particularly noted for its organic fragrances, our scents tend to be more overt and less synthetically layered, making it all the easier for the perfumer to detect the notes."

"So I need to learn the notes first." Adam tipped his head back against his teak lounger and seemed to search the sky. He had removed his dinner jacket and his stark white shirt almost glowed in the pale wash of moonlight that played over them.

"When my mother taught me about scents, she took me in her garden and had me smell everything—the leaves, the petals, the bark of all the trees." The memory washed over Danielle with gentle joy. Her summers with *Maman* at the vacation house in Nice had been filled with painting and playing. Too soon she had realized that not everyone approved of having fun as a worthwhile way to spend time. "Those were the notes for me. Learning to recognize the bouquet of nature."

She sipped her wine, holding a mouthful on her tongue to savor each flavor before simply enjoying the harmony of tastes.

"Danielle, would you excuse me for just a minute?" Adam sprang to his feet, setting his wineglass on the table beside hers. "Literally a minute. No more."

"I will not time you," she declared, amused at his desire for speed. "A French woman does not need a stopwatch to measure increments of life."

"Excuse me." He spun on his heel and stalked away to the stairs leading back down to the main lounge.

Danielle tipped her head back to count the stars, dazzled by the night sky spread above her as if for her pleasure alone. She had barely gotten herself oriented to the constellations when Adam returned, a big bouquet of flowers in hand.

"Oh no." Shaking her head, she smiled. "You did not swipe flowers for a private lesson, did you?"

"I rented them for an hour with twenty bucks and a promise to bring them back." He set the simple glass vase on the table between them, moving the wine bottle to the floor to make room.

"There is not much here aside from roses." Sitting up

to explore the bouquet, she turned so that her feet rested on the floor. "You are familiar with the scent of roses, no?"

"Definitely." He nodded. "But let me take a smell to remind myself."

He leaned in close to the flower and breathed deeply. The vase was packed mostly with pink roses and pink tulips, but there were a few other flowers woven in with the greenery around the edges.

"The bell-shaped flowers are tulips," Danielle said. "Their fragrance is subtle, but we use them sometimes."

"And this?" He held up a sprig of white flowers with greenery.

"That is chamomile."

"Like the tea?"

"Exactly. Although the scent is different when the flowers are fresh."

She identified the remaining blooms and greenery for him and then took another sip of her wine while he sniffed away.

"All right." He closed his eyes. "Test me."

"You think you are ready for a quiz so soon?" She admired his commitment to learn something about the business he represented and wondered if he pursued everything in his life with such intensity.

Now, peering at him in the moonlight, she decided there was something intriguing about a man with his eyes closed. Danielle toyed with the idea of waving her fingers in front of his face to make sure he was not peeking. Or maybe it would be more fun to lean near him, her lips close to his.

The thought sent a shiver down her spine.

HARLEQUIN®

Mediterranean
N I G H T S™

Experience the glamour and elegance of cruising the
high seas with a new 12-book series....

MEDITERRANEAN NIGHTS

Coming in July 2007...

SCENT OF A
WOMAN

by

Joanne Rock

When Danielle Chevalier is invited to an exclusive
conference aboard *Alexandra's Dream*, she knows it
will mean good things for her struggling fragrance
company. But her dreams get a setback when she
meets Adam Burns, a representative from a large
American conglomerate.

Danielle is charmed by the brusque American—
until she finds out he means to compete with her bid
for the opportunity that will save her family business!